BACK TO YOU

KRISTEN GRANATA

MORE FROM KRISTEN

The Collision Series Box Set with Bonus Epilogue
Collision: Book 1
Avoidance: Book 2, Sequel
The Other Brother: Book 3, Standalone
Fighting the Odds: Book 4, Standalone
Hating the Boss: Book 1, Standalone
Inevitable: Contemporary standalone
What's Left of Me: Contemporary standalone
Dear Santa: Holiday novella
Someone You Love: Contemporary standalone

Want to gain access to exclusive news & giveaways?
Sign up for my monthly newsletter!

Visit my website: https://kristengranata.com/
Instagram: https://www.instagram.com/kristen_granata/
Facebook: https://www.facebook.com/kristen.granata.16
Twitter: https://twitter.com/kristen_granata

Want to be part of my KREW?

Join Kristen's Reading Emotional Warriors
A Facebook group where we can discuss my books, books you're reading, and where friends will remind you what a badass warrior you are.

Love bookish shirts, mugs, & accessories?
Shop my book merch shop!

To my inner bitch,
I'm sorry I didn't listen to you sooner.

And to anyone who needs to hear this:
Listen to your gut & follow your heart.
You'll never go wrong as long as you're true to yourself.

PROLOGUE

Christopher

Have you ever forced a smile so hard that it actually hurt?

I think I just pulled a muscle in my face.

Either that or I'm having a stroke. That would give me a good excuse to exit this conversation. *Sorry, I'm having a stroke. I have to go.*

"And then I was like, wait ... is this gluten free? Because I'm gluten intolerant."

What's this girl's name again? My eyes glazed over five minutes ago, yet she continues blabbering on:

"And he was like, "No, ma'am." And I was like, did he just call me ma'am? And then I was like, "I want to speak to your manager.""

Is it Jessica? Or Jamie?

"I mean, how prudent can you be? Can you believe that?"

Maybe it doesn't start with a J at all ...

"Uhm, hello? Are you even listening to me?"

Shit. I've been caught. I clear my throat. "I'm not sure *prudent* is the right word."

Nameless Girl cocks her blond head to the side. "What?"

1

"You said: *How prudent can you be?* But that word doesn't make sense in that sentence."

Her vacant eyes blink back at me.

So I continue to dig my hole deeper. "Prudent means practical, sensible. I think you meant to say *insensitive.*"

Blink, blink.

I lift my half-empty cup of beer to my lips and take a swig. I guess it could be half-full, if you're one of those types. But that's not how I see things. Guess I'm more *prudent.*

My roommate, Damon, claps me on the back. "Hey, man. The pool table's open. Let's go."

I don't play pool, but he's clearly on a search and rescue mission. A damn fine wingman, that friend of mine.

I push my cheeks up, straining through another smile. "I'm going to play pool. It was nice talking to you ..." *Jordana? Jody? Ah, fuck it. Who really cares what her name is?*

She scoffs and rolls her eyes. "Yeah, thanks for the vocabulary lesson."

Damon chokes out a laugh as he ushers me toward the pool table. "Dude, that girl was a sure thing. Tell me you didn't get all nerdy on her."

I shrug before gulping down the rest of my beer. "I don't see what the big deal is. I would want someone to tell me if I used a word incorrectly in a sentence."

He shakes his head. "People don't come to these parties to talk about school. They come here to get fucked up and *not* think about school."

"But a conversation shouldn't be physically painful. Her voice was like nails on a chalkboard. I'm pretty sure she used the word *like* over twelve times within one minute."

Damon leans against the table, leveling me with a look. "That's your problem: You were trying to talk to her. You're supposed to smile and nod, let her run her mouth about whatever she wants. After a few minutes, you ask her if she wants to get out of here. Then, you take her back to your place and fuck her." He spreads his arms out wide. "Have I taught you nothing in the past year?"

I'm quiet as I set my cup down on the edge of the table. It's not socially acceptable for a guy to tell another guy that he's tired of the one-night stands and meaningless conversations. I want to get laid, trust me. But what's wrong with having an interesting conversation with a girl *before* I fuck her? Why can't I enjoy her company, fully-clothed, as much as when we're naked? Is that too much to ask?

That's the *real* foreplay. Getting into a girl's mind before getting into her pants. If I can't stand talking to her, what's going to make me want to fuck her? Stupidity is a major boner killer.

"Earth to Christopher." Damon's waving his hand in front of my face. "There you go, doing that weird disappearing act again." He sighs as he turns around to rack the balls on the table. "I worry about you sometimes."

I grab a pool stick and hold another one out for Damon. "If you think she's so wonderful, why don't you go fuck her yourself?"

He pinches the bridge of his nose. "That's not the point. The chick doesn't have to be *wonderful*. She just needs to have a hole to stick it in."

My stomach rolls at the imagery. "I just don't look at women like that."

Never have. Watching the way my piece of shit father treated my mother solidified that.

Damon leans forward, closing one eye as he lines up his cue to break. "You can't look at every girl like you're choosing a life partner. Not every chick is marriage material, and they know that." His arm shoots forward, scattering the balls around the table, and a striped one rolls into the corner pocket.

It's pointless to argue with him. Our views are too different.

I'm too different.

I walk around the table toward the white ball and bend down, mimicking Damon's stance. I don't know what I'm doing, but I have a clear shot to knock the solid red ball into the side pocket. This should be easy. *Even for me.*

I pump the cue once, twice, and on three I hit the white ball with all my might. It knocks into the red ball like I'd intended, but instead of rolling into the pocket, it flies off the table like a missile.

"Watch out!" I yell.

A dark-haired girl whips around just as the ball reaches her. It slams into her Solo cup, splattering her drink all over her grey hoodie.

"Oh, shit!" Damon covers his mouth with his hand, his shoulders shaking. "Nice one."

I drop my cue and rush over to the poor victim of my inherent clumsiness. *Why does she have to be hot?*

"I'm so sorry. Are you okay?"

She quirks a sleek brow over her black-rimmed glasses. "If by *okay* you mean embarrassed and soaked in beer, then yes. I'm okay."

I grimace, rubbing the back of my neck. "I can't fix the wet part, but I can get you another beer."

Her big brown eyes survey me before she responds. "You mean you're not going to offer me your shirt in a lame attempt to show off your muscular body?"

I glance down at my black T-shirt. "Uh …"

Her lips curve into a smile. "I'm kidding. Keep your shirt on."

Her redheaded friend leans in. "I think some of her beer splashed onto me. I'll take your shirt if she doesn't want it."

Heat creeps into my cheeks. "Let me grab you some napkins."

"That won't be necessary." The brunette turns to her friend and says, "Maybe Brad can give you his shirt, since he's your boyfriend and all."

The redhead pouts. "Joy murderer." Then she spins on her heels and waltzes through the crowd, I assume in search of Brad.

The brunette rolls her eyes, pushing up her glasses with her index finger. Then she extends her hand to me. "Hi, I'm Joy Murderer. It's nice to meet you."

I chuckle and wrap my hand around hers. "Clumsy Chris. The pleasure is mine."

"Is that your given name?"

"Since the second day of first grade."

She clicks her tongue. "That's rough. What'd you do to earn that title?"

"I tripped over my shoelaces and spilled my teacher's coffee all over her blouse."

"Bet you learned how to tie your shoes real quick after that one."

"Ah, but it was too late. The name stuck."

"And followed you all the way to college."

"Pretty sure it'll follow me to my grave."

"They'll put it on your tombstone, no doubt."

I laugh, and this time it isn't forced.

She's beautiful. Long brown hair frames her face, the straight ends almost reaching her elbows. It looks soft, glossy, like the hair on those shampoo commercials. Her skin looks soft too. Pale, but not in that sallow, pasty, creepy-ass vampire kind of way. I hope she wears sunscreen. Down here in Florida, SPF is important.

Why the fuck am I thinking about sunscreen? Maybe Damon's right. Something's wrong with me.

The glasses perched on her nose resemble the black frames I'm currently wearing. She isn't made up like the rest of the girls here. She isn't dressed like them either, who are barely covered up by clothes at all. The grey hoodie she's wearing swallows her body. It looks like ... *oh shit.* It looks like a man's sweatshirt.

"Is that *your* sweatshirt?"

Her head tilts. "Are you implying that I stole it?"

"No, no. I just mean it's, you know, kind of big. I wasn't sure if it was someone else's. Like, a boyfriend or something. I don't think you're a thief. I didn't mean to offend you. I just didn't want to stand here talking to you if ..."

I pause because she's laughing.

"What's so funny?"

"If you want to know if I have a boyfriend, why not come right out and ask me?"

I slip my sweaty hands into my pockets. "I guess I didn't want to seem like a jerk who's only interested in getting into your pants."

Her eyes narrow. "*Are* you interested in getting into my pants?"

"No, not at all," I say too quickly.

Her eyebrows shoot up.

5

"Wait, that came out wrong. I mean, yes, I'd like to get into your pants. You're beautiful. Who wouldn't want to get into your pants? But that's not what I'm trying to do. I just …" I sigh in defeat. "I don't think there's a safe answer to that question."

And she's laughing again.

My cheeks flush. "You're fucking with me, aren't you?"

"I'm sorry. It's just too easy."

I offer her a sheepish grin. "Yeah, I get that a lot."

"You're cute when you're nervous." She pushes up her glasses, locking her eyes on mine. "I don't have a boyfriend."

I nod, my smile spreading wider. "Good to know."

"Do you?"

"Have a boyfriend? No, I don't swing that way."

She giggles, and it's the cutest flutter of sound I've ever heard. "You know what I mean."

"No, I'm single."

"Good. My name's Michelle, by the way."

"Well, Michelle. Can I get you another beer?"

"Sure. Just don't douse me in it this time."

I hold my hands up on either side of my head. "I can't make any promises."

"Guess I'll have to take my chances."

We walk to the nearest keg, and I fill up a new cup. Michelle's fingers brush against mine as she takes her drink from me, warmth sparking and spreading up my arm.

"How come I haven't seen you at any other parties?"

"I'm a freshman." She tips her cup back and takes a sip. "Parties aren't really my thing. I didn't want to come here tonight. That's why I'm trying to disappear inside this big hoodie."

"These parties are kind of …"

"Boring," she finishes.

"Exactly."

She jerks her head toward the door. "Wanna get some air?"

"Sure."

I lead the way, pushing through the sea of people. The closer we get to the makeshift dance floor, the more crowded it gets. I wrap my arm around Michelle's waist, hugging her close to my side. The scent of flowers filters through my nostrils, and I inhale deeper. I like the way she fits in the crook of my arm.

Once we're outside, Michelle points to a cushioned swing at the far end of the backyard. "Let's sit there."

We walk across the grass, stepping around the minefield of red cups and overthrown beer pong balls.

Michelle takes a seat first, crisscrossing her legs. I lower myself beside her, using my long legs to get a gentle rock going.

"Where are you from?" I ask.

"New Jersey. I'm surprised my accent wasn't a dead giveaway."

"It's not bad. You don't sound like Snooki or anything."

She laughs. "You definitely have a southern twang. Are you from around here?"

"Tennessee."

"Why'd you pick Florida?"

"It's where my mom grew up. She always had great things to say about it, so I've always wanted to come see it for myself."

"You said *had*."

I peer up at the starry night sky. "My mom passed away a few years ago."

"I'm sorry I brought it up."

"It's okay. I don't mind talking about her."

"You're better than me," she mutters.

"What does that mean?"

"My mom died when I was twelve. I don't really talk about her much."

"Why not?"

She lifts a shoulder and lets it fall. "I don't know. It still hurts, I guess."

I nod, resisting the urge to reach out for her hand. "I don't think it ever stops hurting."

"How did she die?"

"Breast cancer. What about your mom?"

"Brain tumor."

I shake my head. "The best people are taken too early. Makes you wonder if there's really a God."

"I wonder that all the time." She rests her head back against the cushion. "It'd be nice to think that our moms are up there in Heaven."

I smile. "Maybe they're watching us right now."

"I just want to make her proud."

"I'm sure you already have."

Michelle's dark eyes shimmer in the moonlight when she looks over at me. "I think we're the only two people talking about death at a frat party."

"Trust me, it's still better than the conversation I was trapped in earlier."

"Same," she says, laughing. "I have a hard time connecting with other girls. I grew up with three brothers, so I've always been kind of a tomboy. I don't care much about makeup or fashion."

"I'm more of a video gaming, chess club kind of guy myself."

"Then what are you doing *here*?"

"My roommate begged me to come, and I ran out of excuses."

"Sounds like my roommate. Tanya, the one you met earlier. Her boyfriend's pledging this fraternity so she dragged me along."

"Well, make sure you thank her for me later."

Pink tinges her cheeks. Her doe eyes are stunning, the kind that hold you captive when they land on you. The kind you can't look away from. The kind that look into you and actually see you.

With her eyes on me, there's nothing I wouldn't do for her if she asked.

We swing in the contented quiet with the faint sound of crickets chirping along to the music from the party in the background. We rock and we talk, about everything and nothing.

By the time the night gives way to the morning, I'm in awe of this woman. I've never met someone so real, so honest, so beautiful, inside and out.

The total package.

With heavy eyelids, I drive Michelle back to her dorm and walk her to the entrance of her building.

"I had fun tonight," she says, with a sleepy smile.

"I did too."

The rising sun casts a streak of warm light across her face as we stand facing each other. My insides hum like a beehive, acutely aware of the magnitude of this moment. The overwhelming need to kiss her trumps my nerves, so I lean in, taking her delicate face into my hands.

"I'm not going to sleep with you," she whispers, but doesn't pull away.

"I don't expect you to."

She searches my face, for what I'm not sure. Maybe she's trying to figure out whether or not she can trust me. Whatever she's looking for, I guess she finds it because she closes the gap between us and presses her lips to mine.

And just like that, my entire world tilts on its axis.

Nothing will ever be the same again, and I don't want it to.

Because I'm certain:

I've just met the girl I'm going to spend the rest of my life with.

FIVE YEARS LATER

1

MICHELLE

This is it. The moment I've waited for. The moment four years of college has prepared me for.

Sweaty palms? Check.

Knees? Definitely weak.

Now let's just hope I don't puke on my sweater. I had a burrito bowl for dinner last night. That would be ugly.

The nightmare I'd woken up to around midnight picks this exact moment to resurface: Dozens of piranhas were biting me with their razor-sharp teeth, red eyes gleaming. The weird part was, I wasn't even in the water. They were also a hell of a lot bigger than real piranhas. More like zombie piranhas on steroids. One by one, they attacked, tearing off pieces of my flesh until there was nothing left but bones. I woke up this morning in a cold sweat, screaming at the top of my lungs.

I inhale a shaky breath and replace my thoughts with something positive that one of my favorite professors once said: *The goal of your first day is to survive. Don't expect it to go smoothly. Just get through it.*

With that, I push up my glasses and smile. "Good Morning, class."

"Good Morning, Miss Figueroa."

"I've been so excited to meet all of you. I hope you had a fantastic summer."

My students call out like kernels popping in the microwave:

"I went on vacation!"

"I swam at the beach!"

"I went horseback riding!"

"My dad had a sex change!"

I chuckle, and make a mental note to check in with that last student at some point. "Whoa. I know your kindergarten teachers taught you to raise your hands last year. Let's see who remembers how."

Their hands shoot up.

"Much better. We're all going to share what we did over summer break. But we're going to write about it first."

Some kids cheer, while others groan.

Can't please 'em all. Such is the life of a teacher. It'll be my job for the next 180 days to get those haters to love writing. I'm not worried. I know I can do it.

This is going to be the best first year ever.

After going away to college in Florida, I returned home in search of a job. I'd applied to every elementary school in the state of New Jersey that was within an hour of my house. Lucky for me, I didn't end up having to drive too far. It took me a year, but I landed a first-grade position at a school five minutes away from home. And not just any school: Roosevelt Elementary. The same elementary school I went to as a kid. It doesn't get much better than this.

This is going to be the best first year ever.

The morning flies by and come lunchtime, I'm ravenous. I debate eating in my classroom by myself, but I push that thought away. Socializing with colleagues is an important part of success as a first-year teacher.

Now if only I could find the faculty room. Things look a lot different at your old school when you're adult-sized.

My head is down as I try to find my way using the map the principal handed me earlier this morning, talking aloud to myself.

"There's the gym. There's the library. It must be around here somewhe—"

I smack into something hard. Hula hoops clatter to the floor, bouncing and rolling in opposite directions. I stumble backwards, stunned at the bizarre scene. *Hula hoops?*

"I'm so sorry," a deep voice says. The man turns his back to me, attempting to catch the runaway hoops.

I grab the ones closest to me and stack them on my arm. "I'm the one who should be sorry. I totally wasn't watching where I was going. It's my first day and—"

When he turns around and our eyes meet, I forget how to breathe. Like I've taken a sucker-punch to the gut, all the air is sucked out of my lungs and I'm left reeling from shock.

No. It can't be. There's no way.

"Michelle," he says on an exhale.

Is that my name? I have no idea.

He dips his head down to hold my gaze, which I'm sure has glazed over. "Michelle, what are you doing here?"

Here? Where am I?

My mouth hangs open but I can't close it. The synapses in my brain won't connect. I'll need a cup to drool into when they fit me for my straitjacket and lock me away.

Or maybe I'm just hallucinating. It's a mirage. I had a busy morning. I probably didn't hydrate enough.

There has to be a reasonable explanation because there's no way Christopher *fucking* Hastings is actually standing in front of me right now.

I follow the veins up his forearms, the swell of his biceps. In black basketball shorts and a fitted, gray Under Armor T-shirt, he looks more muscular than I remember. His thick, dark hair looks shinier too. Even his hazel eyes are … hazellier.

He reaches out, brushing his fingers against my shoulder. "Are you okay?"

The contact is exactly what I need. My heart rate kicks up, sending a surge of adrenaline through my veins. Like someone zapped me with a defibrillator, I snap back to life.

"You."

Great, you sound like a caveman.

His eyebrows collapse. "Michelle, I—"

"Why are you in my school?"

The corner of his mouth twitches. "*Your* school?"

"I attended this school when I was a kid. Now I work here. So yes, this is *my* school."

"I work here too." He gestures to his attire. "I'm the Physical Education teacher."

No. Way. "You can't work here. You live in Florida."

Yeah, that's good. Tell him where he lives.

He lifts his large hand to scratch the back of his neck. "I actually haven't lived in Florida in almost five years."

I'm speechless again. My mouth opens and closes while my brain attempts to compute what this means.

Christopher *fucking* Hastings works here.

Here.

At my school.

Where I'll have to see him every day.

Hot tears spring into my eyes, catching me off guard.

Abort! Abort!

I thrust the hula hoops at him and spin around on my heels.

"Michelle, wait."

I don't wait. My body's flight response is better than The Flash himself, and my legs take me far and fast. I don't stop until I'm inside the safety of the bathroom.

I press my back against the door after I close it, chest heaving, squeezing my eyes shut to keep the tears from falling.

"Everything okay?"

I jump at the sound of a man's voice.

Mr. Waters, my very male principal, is staring at me in the reflection of the mirror as he washes his hands.

I clutch my chest. "Why are you in the women's bathroom, sir?"

He yanks out a paper towel and smiles. "I'm not. You're in the men's room."

15

My gaze lands on a row of urinals. "Oh, shit. I mean ... I'm sorry. I didn't mean to curse, sir. I just mean ... I ... I ..."

My brain is apparently short-circuiting.

"Hey, it's okay," he says, walking toward me. "It's my first day too. Are you all right?"

I release a breath between my lips. "I was just looking for the faculty room."

He jerks his thumb to the left. "It's next door."

Of course it is. "Oh."

"I just had to call a mother to let her know that her son smeared his feces all over the bathroom stall. Think of it this way: Your day can't be worse than hers." Mr. Water grimaces. "Or the poor bastard that has to clean it."

I'd take the shit smears over the man I just ran into.

I force a smile and nod. "Thank you, sir." Then I slip out the door and speed-walk to my classroom.

I was wrong this morning. Very wrong.

This is going to be the worst *first year ever.*

CHRISTOPHER

So many nights I'd tossed and turned in bed, tortured by the memory of what I'd almost had. What I'd never have again.

Until now.

She's here.

I can't believe it.

She hates me.

That I can believe.

Can't say I blame her either. I hate myself for what I did.

Even if it was the best thing for her.

When I'd gone away to college, I swore that I'd never see my family again. Why would I? I was going to make a better life for myself. One that didn't involve my alcoholic father or my drug addict sister. Mom was the only real family I'd had, and her death was the knife that severed any ties I had to a home.

So I left Tennessee behind to start a new life in Florida.

The three months I'd spent with Michelle were the best three months of my life. In those three months, I saw our future together so clearly. I was convinced we'd be together forever.

Then the rug was pulled out from under me. Unfortunately, the distance I'd put between me and my reject family didn't shake them off me for good. I guess it doesn't matter how far you go. Family knows no bounds.

It killed me to leave Michelle like I did. Life always makes you choose between doing what you really want to do, and doing the right thing. Why the two can't be synonymous, I'll never understand. Maybe it is for some people.

But for whatever reason, the universe sent Michelle back to me. Right to this very school. This isn't just a coincidence.

It's fate.

After everything I've been through, I deserve it, don't I?

Sure, Michelle bolted after our encounter this morning, but that's okay. She's stuck working with me for the next 180 days. I'm going to do whatever I can to make it up to her. To right my wrongs.

This is my chance. My shot at a normal life. At getting the girl. Things are finally looking up for me.

This is going to be the best year *ever*.

After the dismissal bell rings, I make a beeline to Michelle's classroom. It's the end of the first day, and I know she won't be in a rush to leave. Most teachers stay late to organize their classrooms and prepare for the next day.

I step into the doorway of her room, but my hand stills mid-air before knocking. Michelle has her back to me, her long hair now swept into a messy bun.

What I wouldn't give to wrap my arms around her and run my nose along the soft nape of her neck.

Her pencil skirt hugs her curves, prompting the memory of our last night together to replay in my mind. The way her hips moved in sync with mine, the sounds she made in my ear, the way it felt to be inside her ...

"Are you lost?"

I blink as Michelle glares at me from across the room.

Shit. She just caught me ogling her like a Neanderthal. The semi in my pants will *not* help my case while I'm trying to win her over.

And sporting a boner in an elementary school is extremely dangerous for my career.

I clear my throat. "Uh, h-hi. How was your first day?"

Her eyebrow arches. "My day was fine. And the last five years of my life have been fine too, not that you would know."

I cringe. "I know you hate me."

"Glad we cleared that up. You can go now."

My feisty girl.

I stride into her room, confident and ready to spill it all. But my foot rolls over a pencil on the floor, and I stumble into a desk. A stack of paper tips over, the white sheets fanning out onto the floor. I rush forward in an attempt to catch them, but end up kicking over the garbage can. I fall forward, used tissues littering the tile around me like a booger-filled chalk outline as I hit the floor with a thud.

It's a domino effect of utter stupidity.

I close my eyes and grit my teeth. *Smooth move, you idiot.*

Michelle's giggling flutters around me. When I open my eyes, her hand clamps over her mouth and her shoulders shake.

"Come on," I say, gesturing with my hands. "You can let it out. I know you're dying to."

Her laugh bursts free as she bends at the waist and places her hands on her knees for support.

"I'll clean all this up," I say.

This incites more laughter. Michelle is full-blown belly laughing and I'm loving every second of it. I know she's laughing at my expense, but at least she's laughing. Laughter is better than anger. I can work with this.

She lifts her glasses and wipes her eyes. "I'm sorry. I guess I forgot how clumsy you are."

"A lot of things have changed over the years, but unfortunately that isn't one of them."

She sobers at that, and I consider tripping over something else to keep her laughing.

She kneels down to clean up the mess and I crouch down beside her. "Let me do it. I'm the one who just trashed your room."

"It's fine," she snaps. "I've got it."

One step forward, two steps back.

In silence, we reorganize the papers into a neat pile and sweep the garbage back into the trashcan.

I offer Michelle my hand when I stand. She slips her small hand into mine, and when she does, I'm blinded by the sparkling diamond that adorns her ring finger.

My heart stalls out.

My blood runs cold.

No. She can't be.

She pulls her hand back and crosses her arms over her chest, stuffing the offending hand into the crook of her elbow. "You said it yourself: A lot has changed."

The balloon of hope that'd filled inside me this morning has been pricked with a pin. All of the air whooshes out of me.

How foolish I was to expect someone like her to be single after all these years. Of course she wouldn't still love me, still pining away the way I have. I broke her heart. She deserves better. Better than me.

She always has.

Still, I swallow past the boulder lodged in my throat, wanting to set the record straight regardless. "I just came here to say—"

Her hand flies up, palm facing me. "Please, save your excuses. I don't care to hear them."

"But if you would hear me out—"

"I don't want to hear you out, Christopher." She spits my name like it's poison on her tongue. "You don't deserve to have me listen to you. You've had five years to reach out to me. Five years to answer my texts. Five years to let me know that you were even alive, or that you weren't abducted by aliens. Do you know how worried I was? Do you know what it feels like to have someone you care about literally vanish from your life as if he never existed?"

My shoulders slump and I shake my head. "No, but I do know what it feels like to have to walk away from the one person I wanted more than anything."

Her expression softens for a millisecond before her hardened mask replaces it. "Please, just leave me alone."

I want to apologize, tell her everything. But she's so closed off, I'm not sure she'd accept anything I say in this moment. Would it even matter if she knew the truth?

She loves someone else now.

Within just a few hours, I've found her and lost her, all over again.

* * *

After leaving Michelle's room, dragging my defeated heart behind me, I high-tail it over to the middle school.

As usual, I'm enslaved by the manacles of obligation.

Okay, maybe that's a little dramatic. But it's true.

I slow to a stop in the fire lane at the side entrance of the building. Leaving my keys in the ignition, I jog to the door and tap my knuckles against it.

Mrs. Holly swings open the door and greets me with a warm smile. "Good Afternoon, Mr. Hastings. How are you?"

"I'm great, thanks. How's my boy doing today?"

Mrs. Holly lifts her wrinkled hand and points toward the far end of the cafeteria. "He's been reading since he got here. He's really into that book."

A surge of pride swells in my chest. "He goes through them like water. It's a battle every night to get him to put down the book and go to bed."

She laughs, her skin crinkling around the corners of her crystal-blue eyes. "There are worse things in life."

"Yes, there are."

I'm well-aware.

I walk up behind Aiden, taking in his frail body as I ruffle his dark hair. It's crazy how much he looks like I did when I was his age.

"Hey, yyyou're mmmessing it up," he slurs, feigning annoyance despite his crooked smile.

I hold my hands up. "Sorry. Though I don't see how it looks much different now than it did before I messed it up. You sure you're not ready for a haircut yet?"

He shakes his head. "Nnno. I told yyyou, I'm grrrowing it out."

I lift his backpack and sling it over my shoulder, hoping he doesn't get mad. I've seen all the other parents here do the same for their kids. "Fine. But you're shampooing tonight. I think there's a family of mice scampering around in there."

A toothy grin brightens Aiden's face. "Is nnnot. I just wwwashed it on Tuesday."

He musters all of his strength to lift himself off the bench. One of his forearm crutches clatters to the ground. Instinctually, I bend down to grab it.

"I don't nnneed help," Aiden says. "I can do it on mmmy own."

I heave a sigh. "I'm just using my manners. I'd do it for anybody who dropped something, not just you."

It pains me to stand idly by while Aiden struggles, but I understand why he fights for his independence. Cerebral Palsy is debilitating enough. It separates him from the rest of his peers. If there's something he can do on his own, despite how long it takes him or how much it might hurt, he's going to do it. I admire the shit out of him for that.

He's the strongest person I know.

We say goodbye to Mrs. Holly and make our way to my car. I slow my pace as inconspicuously as I can while Aiden leans on his crutches to swing his uncoordinated legs.

"Yyyou're in a bad mmmood. What's wrrrong?"

Perceptive kid. I thrust my fingers through my hair and blow a stream of air between my lips. "Today's been a crazy day."

"Wwwhy?"

"Do you remember that girl I told you about? The one I was with at college before I came back to live with you?"

Aiden nods, stopping at the curb.

"Well, she showed up at my school today. She's working there."

His eyebrows lift, his left one higher than his right. "Wwwow. She lives here nnnow?"

I swing open the passenger door for him and walk around my front bumper. "She's always lived here. She only went to Florida for college."

Aiden's quiet until we're buckled and on our way home. "Is that why you wwwanted to mmmove here? Because of her?"

"Among other things." I need to choose my words carefully

with him.

"Wwwas she happy to see yyyou?"

Michelle's beautiful, scowling face flashes through my mind. "No. No, she wasn't."

"What are yyyou gonna do?"

"Nothing. She's engaged." The words are a dagger to my bleeding heart. "There's not much I can do."

Aiden's eyes are on me as I drive. "Do yyyou still love her?"

Warmth spills out over my body. "I do. I think I always will."

"So fight for her."

I shake my head. "She's marrying someone else, bud."

"But she's nnnot mmmarried yet. You fought for mmme, remember? Yyyou said wwwe don't abandon the ones we love."

I glance at Aiden out of the corner of my eye, surprised he remembers that after all these years. "This is different. I *did* abandon her, and she hates me for it."

"Does she know wwwhy yyyou left?"

I shake my head. "She doesn't want to hear it."

He thinks for a minute before asking, "What's her favorite snnnack?"

"She always loved donuts. Why do you ask?"

"Yyyou should buy her a donnnut and tell her you wwwant to be friends."

I click the blinker and roll to a stop as I approach the stop sign. "I don't know if I can be her friend. Watch her marry someone else." My throat tightens. "It would be too hard."

"You're nnnot going to be her friend. You're going to trrry to wwwin her back. But she doesn't have to knnnow that."

I laugh. "And when did you become the love guru?"

"I just knnnow lots of things."

I reach over and squeeze his knee. "Yeah, you do."

"What are wwwe having for dinner?" he asks.

"Do you want leftovers or pizza?"

"Is that evennn a question?"

I check my blind spot and cut over to make a quick right turn. "Pizza it is."

2

MICHELLE

"I wouldn't do that if I were you."

I scribble my name onto the sign-up sheet and return the pen to Beth, the school secretary. "I'm the newbie. I have to sign up for everything."

Beth slips her glasses off and gives me a hard stare. "That game is dangerous."

"It's just dodgeball."

She leans in, motioning for me to do the same, and her voice lowers to a whisper. "These teachers play dirty. Don't let their smiles fool you."

I shrug. "I've got three brothers. Nothing scares me."

Beth shakes her head. "Don't say I didn't warn you."

A pretty blond woman bursts into the main office. She stalks past me in her heels and into the principal's office, slamming the door behind her.

Beth bustles around the desk and pulls my arm until we're standing outside the door. She presses her ear against it.

"Why are we eavesdropping?" I whisper.

"Something's going on with those two," Beth says. "They've been at each other's throats."

I raise an eyebrow but keep my mouth shut. The last thing I need is to get caught up in the school gossip.

"She's mad because he signed her up for the dodgeball game," Beth whispers.

"Can he do that? It's a voluntary event."

"He's the boss. He can do whatever he wants."

Principal Waters seems so kind. It's hard to imagine him forcing a teacher to play in the dodgeball charity game.

Beth and I scurry away from the principal's door when the door to the main office swings open.

My heart falters when Christopher waltzes in. His signature basketball shorts and T-shirt stretch around his toned body.

If only I could forget what that body looks like underneath the clothes.

But his broad shoulders, smooth chest, and shredded, lean stomach are forever burned into my memory. As is the feel of his strong arms wrapped around me, the way his fingers interlaced with mine, the taste of his kiss.

My skin flushes, heat stealing up my neck. I'd spent four years hating him, yet I'm still overcome with desire the second he walks into a room. It's like my heart and my vagina staged a coup against my poor, defenseless brain.

I'd tried to fight the instant attraction when I first met Christopher. My guard was up. Beautiful boys break hearts. Still, he'd weaseled his way inside, and not like the cute dog who ends up on the couch after you've told him not to. No, Christopher *fucking* Hastings was a Trojan horse. Just when I'd started to fall for him, vulnerable and blind, he slit my throat as I slept and disappeared into the night.

"My two favorite ladies," Christopher says. "Good Morning."

My eyes narrow when he flashes that dimpled smile.

He is the enemy, dimples be damned.

Beth winks. "Good Morning, good lookin'."

A frustrated screech sounds from inside the principal's office before the door flies open and the blond teacher stomps out.

Christopher points to the dodgeball sign-up, oblivious to her bad mood. "Hey, Raegan. It's awesome that you signed up for the dodgeball game. The kids will be so excited."

Her cheeks turn a deep shade of red. "Ugh!" She spins around and clomps out into the hallway.

Beth and I exchange glances.

Christopher holds his hands up on either side of his head. "Was it something I said?"

I snort. "Seems to be the affect you have on women."

Principal Waters exits his office wearing a smug smile. "Good Morning, everyone."

"Good Morning, sir." I gesture to the sign-up sheet. "I'm looking forward to the dodgeball game."

"You're playing?" Christopher asks.

I give him a curt nod, an attempt at playing nice in front of the boss.

A wide grin spreads across Christopher's face. "Man, I'm putting you on my team."

My eyebrows shoot up. "*Your* team?"

"I'm the team captain. I play every year."

Of course he does. The guy can throw a dodgeball, but he can't lift the phone to call me.

I roll my eyes and I breeze past him as the morning bell rings.

To my chagrin, he jogs behind me in the hallway to catch up. "If you want, I'll put you on the opposing team. This way you can launch as many balls at my head as you want."

"Tempting."

He twists his backpack in front of him and pulls out a brown paper bag. "I got your favorite."

Dunkin Donuts.

Oh, he's playing dirty. How am I supposed to resist chocolate sugary glaze drizzled over chocolate spongy cake?

Adam caved over a measly apple, but we're talking about donuts, here!

I speed up my stride to take me away from him *and* the delicious scent of sweet dough. Coming from Christopher, they're more like *Devil's Donuts.*

In a second, he's beside me again. "You know you want it."

"I don't want anything from you."

He dangles the bag in front of my face. "Come on, Bambi."

A shooting pain stabs my heart, quickly followed by anger. "You don't get to call me that anymore."

"I'm sorry. Please, just take the donut. Can't we at least be friends?"

"You want to be *friends?*"

An explosion goes off in my brain. I rip the bag out of his hand and waltz over to our custodian. "Hey, Gary. My *friend* Christopher got you this. He wants your number but he's too shy to ask for it."

Gary, who looks to be about sixty-five, lifts a bushy eyebrow. "Uh … thanks. But I'm married."

Christopher stammers, eyes wide, trying to explain.

And I turn into my classroom with a victorious smile, despite the fact that I just wasted a perfectly good donut.

* * *

"How's work?"

I stuff a forkful of spaghetti into my mouth. "Good."

Dad's eyebrows raise. "That's riveting information."

I giggle around the mouthful of carbs. "My class is great. The kids are so sweet. I like my principal. It's his first year at our school so it's nice to know I'm not the only new one."

"He's young for a principal, isn't he?" my older brother, Michael, asks.

"I think he's in his thirties."

"Nothing wrong with that," Dad says.

My younger brother, Ryan, strides into the dining room, carrying a basket of dinner rolls.

Caleb, the youngest out of us, holds his hands up in front of his face. "Pass me a roll."

Ryan tosses it at him, hard. "Use your manners, dipshit."

Dad shakes his head. "Can't we have one normal meal?"

Caleb tears a piece of bread off with his teeth, reminiscent of a lion eating a carcass. "What? This is normal for us."

Ryan smacks the back of Caleb's head. "Don't talk with your mouth full."

Caleb swats Ryan's arm. "Don't make me choke, asswipe."

Ryan twists Caleb's wrist, and in the blink of an eye, the two are wrestling on the floor.

Michael and I exchange glances. There's no use in stopping them. We've tried.

I stab a meatball with my fork. "I signed up for a dodgeball game. It's a charity event. My school raises money for underprivileged kids in our community."

"Couldn't you do something a little less dangerous for charity?" Dad asks.

I wink. "Don't worry. I'll go easy on 'em."

Michael laughs. "Remember when you went through that wrestling phase? You used to stuff mom's bra with tissues and jump off the couch onto a pile of pillows."

Dad's belly shakes as he chuckles. "We were wondering where all the tissues were going."

"Yeah, and you all blamed me," Ryan says, stepping over Caleb as he takes his seat at the table again.

"Oh, I was convinced it was you," Dad says, tipping his cup toward Ryan. "No one used as many tissues as you did."

I snort. "You jerked off so much, I thought your dick was going to fall off."

Caleb groans, curled up in a ball on the floor, clutching his side. "Ry, I think you ruptured my spleen."

"Your spleen isn't on that side, you idiot." Michael shakes his head.

"When's this charity game?" Dad asks. "I'd love to come watch you play."

"Next week." I take a long sip of my Pinot Noir. "Wednesday night."

"I'm off Wednesday night, but I can't make it." Michael sits back, a slow smile creeping onto his face. "I've got a date."

We all hoot and holler, causing the color in Michael's cheeks to redden.

"Finally asked her out, huh?" Dad asks.

"Asked her last night at the end of our shift."

"What was her reaction?" I ask.

"She asked me what took me so long."

I bark out a laugh. "Told you she was into you."

Michael leans over and digs his knuckles into my scalp. "My baby sister is always right."

I duck out of his reach. "Get off the hair, you freak."

Caleb crawls back to his chair. "Now we've all got someone. All except you, Dad."

Dad holds his ring finger in the air, pointing to his wedding band. "My heart is taken forever."

Ryan sighs. "Mom's been gone for twelve years. Don't you think you need to find someone to spend the remainder of your life with?"

"Remainder?" Dad's mouth hangs open. "You say it like I'm about to die."

"You're not. Death is a long time away. That's why you need to find someone."

"Not happening." Dad turns his attention back to me. "Speaking of, where's Richard tonight?"

Thanks for throwing me under the bus, Dad. "He's stuck at work."

"Again?" Michael asks.

"He's one busy Dick." Caleb snorts, cracking himself up.

Dad sends a pointed glare his way. "His name is Richard."

"He's working on an important case," is all I say.

"That's the life of a lawyer." Michael says it simply, but I know there's nothing simple behind his meaning.

My family knows very little about my relationship with Richard, and I like it that way. The less contact they have with him the better. Three overbearing brothers and an overprotective father aren't exactly the best welcoming committee. More like a firing squad. Case in point: Senior Prom. Michael hid in the bushes outside the house, and when my date attempted to kiss me goodnight, Michael tossed him down the porch steps.

Being the only female can be a challenge at times. Those are the times I miss Mom the most.

It still saddens me to talk about her. Actually, Christopher was the only person I'd ever opened up to. He was able to relate, being that he'd lost his mom too.

My heart squeezes as I recall the connection we'd shared. What happened? What made him vanish seemingly into thin air? Why didn't he reach out to me? Did he miss me as much as I missed him?

For years, questions plagued me, until I had to stuff them inside a box and throw away the key. I had to move on. I never expected to get answers. Never expected to see him again. Now, the dusty old box has popped open, and all those questions are swirling around me. Christopher's here, and he can finally give me the answers I've wanted for so long.

The ironic thing is: I'm not so sure I'm ready for them. What difference would they make anyway?

I'm marrying Richard.

After dinner, Michael and I head to the kitchen for dish duty.

"You okay?" he asks.

I grab the sponge and start washing our sauce-filled bowls. "Yeah, why?"

"You're quiet."

"Oh, I'm just tired from work."

"Everything okay with Richard?"

"Yep."

"You know you can talk to me, right?"

I scrunch my nose. "About boys? Thanks, but I'll pass."

He takes a pot from me and swipes the towel around it. "Not about what you *do* with boys." He pauses to make a dramatic show of shuddering. "But you can talk to me about your life. About what's going on. Ask me for advice."

I peer up at him out of the corner of my eye. "You're the one who comes to me for advice, remember?"

"The student can become the teacher, you know. Try me."

I chew the inside of my cheek, mulling it over. "Okay, fine."

"Seriously?"

"Sure." I wave a knife in his direction, droplets of water splattering onto his shirt. "But if you tell Dad or the boys, I will gut you in your sleep."

Michael holds his hands up on either side of his head. "I won't say a word."

Here goes. "I met someone Freshman year at college. Christopher. We had this instant chemistry. We hung out every day, talked for hours. It was like we were best friends, except we were more."

"That sounds perfect."

I nod, rinsing the suds off a bowl before handing it to Michael. "I'd made him wait a few months before ... before we ... you know."

"Yes, my little sister had sex. Keep the story moving."

"After all that waiting, we spent the night together. It was a defining moment, like it'd sealed our fates somehow. I believed we'd always be together."

Michael's knuckles turn white as he grips the bowl. "So what happened?"

My mind wanders back in time, drudging up the painful memory of that morning ...

A SMILE STRETCHES MY LIPS BEFORE I EVEN OPEN MY EYES.

Visions of last night dance in my mind. Last night was ... wow. My body aches in the best way, sore in all the right spots. Sex has never been like that before. And something tells me it'll never be like that with anyone else.

He's different.

And to think this whole thing started at a frat party I didn't want to go to. I'd rebelled, of course, wearing baggy jeans and a hoodie, much to my roommate's dismay. If I was being dragged into frat boy hell against my will, I was determined to be comfortable while I died a slow and painful death.

I'd never expected to meet a guy there—a guy I actually liked. One who wasn't searching for his next conquest or funneling beer through his ass hole.

Aside from the fact that he'd assaulted me with a pool ball, we hit it off right away. On the outside, he looked like a typical jock: Tall, muscular, a thick head of lush dark hair. But on the inside? Total nerd. He's the best of both worlds: The good guy who looks like a bad guy. If I got to build my own man, Weird Science-style, he'd be who stepped out of the computer.

Christopher Hastings.

Even his name is sexy.

Despite my body's physical reaction to him the night we kissed, I'd made him wait three months before we had sex. I had to be sure. I had to know he was worth giving it up for. Guys are so desperate for a warm hole to stick it in, they'll say anything to convince you to let them.

But not Christopher. He never pressured me once. And last night, I finally let him in.

Figuratively and literally.

My hand slides across the mattress, reaching for him, eager to feel the warmth of his body against mine as we wake up together.

The sheets on his side of the bed are cool to the touch. My eyelids flutter open and it takes a minute for my vision to register in the darkness before the green numbers on the digital clock click into focus.

5:30AM.

Maybe he left early for class.

Three hours early? No way.

Okay, maybe he's in the kitchen cooking breakfast for me.

That only happens in romance novels. Don't delude yourself. He snuck out in the middle of the night.

I flip the covers off my legs and roll out of bed, determined to prove my inner bitch wrong. Wrapping my fuzzy robe around my midsection, I shuffle into the hallway. The bathroom door is ajar, lights are off. Further down the hall, my fingers feel around for the light switch. The kitchen lights flip on, illuminating the harsh truth.

Told you, he left.

"You don't know that," I grumble as I pad back to my bedroom.

Christopher is just as romantic as those fictional boyfriends. He's probably out grabbing coffee right now. He knows how much I love Dunkin in the morning.

What if he hated last night? What if you sucked so bad in bed that he ran away after you fell asleep?

I huff out a laugh and roll my eyes. That's ridiculous. The four orgasms he had made it obvious that he loved last night as much as I did.

So where is he then?

Back in my bed, I scoot under the comforter and bring my phone with me. No new texts or calls. My thumbs fly across the screen as I type out a text asking Christopher where he went and then hit Send. But after staring at the screen for thirty minutes, dread pools in my stomach.

I take a shower, get dressed, and make myself a bowl of cereal. I busy myself with mundane things around the apartment to stop myself from checking my phone. Then it's time to head out to class.

Alone.

I sling my backpack on my shoulder and walk as quickly as I can to school, hoping to see Christopher's smiling face when I get there.

Forget about him. He's gone.

He's not gone. He cares about me.

He waited until he got what he wanted from you.

He's not like that.

All guys are the same.

He's different. I'm falling in love with him.

He got the milk for free and now he's gone. You got used.

"Shut up!" I scream.

A group of girls walking beside me jump at my insane outburst, surveying me with wide eyes. I stride ahead of them as they giggle and whisper about the "crazy girl" talking to herself.

Tears well as I turn toward the Education building.

Don't cry. He's not worth it.

But he is. I felt it.

Christopher doesn't show up to class, but I continue to give him the benefit of the doubt for the remainder of the day. Something has to be wrong. He wouldn't disappear like this without telling me. I grow more nervous by the hour.

But one day turns into two, and two days turn into a week. My texts and calls go unanswered. His roommate doesn't know where he is either, or at least he's not telling me.

The longer I wait, the more everything becomes clear.

Christopher really is gone.

My inner bitch was right.

And I hate when she's right ...

. . .

I shut the lever on the faucet and turn to face Michael. "We were together for three months straight, and then he was just gone. He disappeared, as if he never existed at all." I bite my bottom lip to stop it from quivering.

Michael's expression darkens. "That's odd."

"But here's the clincher: He works at my school now. I bumped into him on the first day. Just like that, he's back in my life. Here, of all places."

"Wow. What did he say when he saw you?"

"He tried explaining himself, but I wouldn't hear him out."

"Why not?"

I shrug. "I really don't want to hear some lame excuse as to why he left. It's been years, Michael. I've moved on." I glance down at my beautiful engagement ring, the reminder of just how far I've pushed myself to move on.

"Aren't you curious though? Shit, I'm curious and I just heard a snippet of the story."

I shake my head. "It's not like it'll erase what he did."

The years of quiet heartache.

The nights I'd cried myself to sleep.

The barrier I'd put up around my heart so no one could ever hurt me like that again.

"But it might give you closure. It might help to know why he left. Maybe it has nothing to do with you."

"What could possibly be the reason that you can't even send a simple text? Email me, stick a postcard in the mail, send an owl. Something."

He sighs. "Sometimes in life, you think you're making the right decision, and at the time, it seems like your only option. Kind of like you and Richard."

I cross my arms over my chest. "What's *that* supposed to mean?"

"You know Richard isn't right for you, yet you're forcing it anyway."

My mouth drops open. "You don't know what you're talking about. You don't even know Richard that well."

"Exactly, Mich." He rests his hands on my shoulders. "I don't know him because he's never around to get to know. And I think you're the reason why that is. You're purposely keeping him away from us because you don't want us to see what you already know."

I pull out of his grasp. "We are in love and we are getting married. Richard is a nice guy. He's smart, he's dependable."

"You just explained all the great qualities of a Labrador."

"Well, what's wrong with that? Everyone loves Labradors." I lift my arms and let them smack down at my sides. "Why don't you want to see your sister happy?"

Michael leans his hip against the counter. "I do want to see you happy, Mich. That's why I'm telling you the truth: Richard isn't right for you. And maybe this guy from college is back in your life for a reason."

I roll my eyes. "Oh, yes. You're right. It's a sign from the universe telling me to break up with Richard."

"Is that so crazy? The guy just so happens to work at the same school where you got hired. That's not random. And he clearly still cares about you after all this time, otherwise he wouldn't be trying to explain himself to you. That sounds like the universe at work to me."

I plant my hands on my hips. "What happened to the big brother who launched Travis Speedman off the porch for trying to kiss me after prom? Why are you taking Christopher's side and not mine?"

"I'm always on your side. That's why I'm telling you to hear him out. I think it'll be good for you to hear it, at the very least." He grins. "And if he gives you a dumbass story? I'll kick his ass."

A smile cracks through my façade. "You promise?"

"I promise, little sis'."

3

MICHELLE

Water droplets slide down my bare skin as I pad down the hallway.

Richard's been so busy with his latest case at work, we've barely spent any time together in the past few weeks. His hours often fluctuate depending on the needs of his clients, but the pressure to make partner at his firm has recently sent him into overdrive.

Tonight, though, he's home at a reasonable hour. So I took a shower after clearing our dinner plates away, giving him time to work in his home office—where I'm now standing in the doorway.

Naked.

You shouldn't be this nervous to fuck your fiancé.

It's been a while. Plus, I don't want to disturb him. He gets angry when I interrupt him.

He should welcome the interruption of his naked fiancé.

He just needs some persuasion. Hence the nakedness. I tap my knuckles against the doorframe, exhaling the nerves through my nostrils.

Richard glances up from his computer screen. Over the rim of his glasses, his pale-blue eyes skate over my exposed body. "Well, this is a nice surprise."

His hand's still on the mouse. He should be standing up, stalking toward you, taking you.

He's just caught off guard. He needs a second to register what I'm doing.

You're naked. You're obviously not here for a soccer match.

"I thought you might want to take a break from work."

Richard's gaze moves from me to the computer screen.

He shouldn't be able to take his eyes off you.

"I'm really swamped, babe. Raincheck?"

My arms wrap around my waist as if I can physically shield myself from the rejection. "Oh, sure. Just figured you'd want to release some tension. I didn't mean to bother you."

You sound pathetic.

Richard leans back in his leather chair, tossing his glasses onto the desk. "You know what? I can't say no to you." He gestures with his finger. "Come here."

I give him a sly smile. See? Just needed some persuasion.

On what planet do guys need to be persuaded to have sex?

I shut my inner bitch out as I 'round the corner of the desk and bend down to meet his lips with mine.

The sound of his zipper echoes in the quiet room. I lift my leg, but his hands push against my waist to stop me from straddling him.

"I'll get you later," he says, slipping his erection out of his boxers. "I just need to finish up in here first."

But he has time for you to suck him off?

"Oh, of course." I lower myself to my knees on the cold hard-wood floor. I swallow my pride, past the lump in my throat, before taking his length into my mouth.

His hands remain on the armrests of his chair, instead of fisting handfuls of my hair.

He barely makes a sound, instead of groaning in ecstasy.

Going down on Richard definitely puts the *job* in *blowjob*.

In what feels like a matter of seconds, Richard pulses his release. Then he pats me on my ass when I stand, and swivels his chair to face the computer again. "Thanks babe. I'll meet you in the bedroom soon."

I blink back the water brimming at the surface of my lids and scurry down the hall, locking myself in the bathroom. The click of the doorknob signals the release of my tears.

Staring at my reflection in the mirror above the sink, I square my shoulders and give myself a mental slap.

Don't cry. You wanted this. Your tears are pointless.

Prior to September, I hadn't cried in five years—not since Christopher disappeared. I'd cried enough then to last me a lifetime.

Then I met Richard at a bar after I'd returned home from college. He was blunt, cut-and-dry, looking at life like a spreadsheet. Everything belonged in a column. Everything was simple. Logical. Death, disease, work, money, family, friendship. They were all the same to him.

Having been burned from all-consuming love and passion, I found comfort in Richard's emotionless outlook. So I swore I'd never let another man make me cry again. I took a page out of Pat Benatar's book and hardened my heart.

Yet tonight makes three times my emotions have gotten past my defenses in the last week.

What's going on with me?

Richard doesn't make you happy.

Yes, he does. We're getting married.

That doesn't mean you're happy.

He's a good guy.

Doesn't make him the right *guy for you.*

I wipe my eyes with the backs of my hands and force myself to ignore the doubt and the pain. If I ignore it, it doesn't exist.

Richard said he'd meet me in the bedroom, so I wait there for him. Busying myself, I pick out my outfit for work for the following day, put the laundry away, and read a chapter on my Kindle. Just as my eyes close, the mattress dips down.

Richard pecks my forehead. "Goodnight, babe."

"Wait, I'm up." My hand reaches out for him.

He chuckles. "Your eyes are still closed. You're tired. Get some rest."

Forcing myself up, I scoot back against the headboard. "I'll sleep when I'm dead."

"Work's been taking a lot out of you, huh?"

I nod, stifling a yawn. "The first week was crazy. I need to get into my groove."

"You will."

"Speaking of work, I volunteered to play in a dodgeball game for charity. It's next Wednesday. I'd love it if you came to watch."

"I have an important meeting with a client on Wednesday."

"You don't even know what time the game is."

He turns toward me, sighing as he pushes his glasses up onto his forehead. "What time is the game?"

"Six o'clock."

He shakes his head. "No can do, babe."

My bottom lip juts out. "Can't you just move the appointment around?"

"No, I can't. This case is important, Michelle."

"My job's important too, you know."

He rolls his eyes. "It's not the same. A dodgeball game doesn't compare to a judicial case."

I understand his way of thinking, in the literal sense. But it's not just about the dodgeball game. It's about what the dodgeball game represents: Me. My career. My wants. My needs.

None of which seem to come first on Richard's spreadsheet.

"What's going to happen when we have a kid? What happens when he or she is in a school play or the science fair?"

Richard shrugs. "Then you'll go to those events. That's what moms do."

And with that, he leans over and turns off the lamp on his night-stand, thus ending the conversation.

If only there was a similar switch for my feelings.

CHRISTOPHER

"I'm up. I'm up."

I rip the covers off and swing my legs out of bed.

After riding the bus last week, Aiden's been begging me to drive him to school.

"The aisle is too nnnarrow for my crrrutches, and the other kids starrre at me," he'd said. How could I say no to that?

Now I'm waking up an hour earlier than usual to ensure that I can get the both of us to school on time.

"Sommmething's definitely up," Aiden says.

I look down at my pitched boxers and quickly pull my pillow onto my lap. "You have one of these. You know what it's like when you wake up."

Aiden smirks as he makes his way into the hallway. "When wwwas the last time yyyou got laid?"

I toss the pillow at him, but it smacks against the doorframe due to my outstanding lack of aim. "Why don't you make yourself useful and start the Keurig for me."

"Already mmmade your coffee," he calls from down the hall. "Scrammmbled eggs and bacon are donnne too."

"You're the best twelve-year old I know."

25

"I'm the onnnly twelve-year old yyyou know."

I thank my lucky stars every day that this kid's a boy. We can joke about morning wood and I can talk to him about the birds and the bees because we have the same parts. I wouldn't have known what to do with a girl. Especially a teenage girl. I shudder at the thought as I twist the knob on the shower all the way to hot.

Aiden's not wrong about getting laid. It feels like it's been forever. Definitely well over a year now. Raising a kid on your own kind of puts a damper on dating, but I can't use that as an excuse. I've tried to put myself out there and meet women. None of them lasted very long. My heart's just not in it.

It belongs to someone else.

I'm afraid it always will.

Just the thought of Michelle tempts me to wrap my hand around my dick and give myself some relief. But knowing she now belongs to someone else ruins the fantasy.

So I switch the temperature of the water to cold and rinse off.

"Yyyou stopping for donuts?" Aiden asks when we get into my car.

I shake my head.

"Commme on. Yyyou can't let the other guy steal yyyour girl."

"He didn't steal her. He got her fair and square."

"Yyyou had her first."

I chuckle. "Life doesn't work like that, bud."

"Life worrrks however yyyou make it work. Grown-ups are the ones who commmplicate everrrything."

I glance over at him. "You're pretty philosophical, you know that?"

"Mmmy teacher says I'm an old soul."

Guilt trickles into the pit of my stomach. Aiden had to grow up way too quickly being raised by his junkie mother. Seen things no little kid should've seen. I've heard some of the stories, but I can't begin to imagine the extent of it. He's so mature for someone so young.

Which is why he doesn't need to be burdened with my problems.

"Why don't you see if Jordan wants to see a movie this weekend? He can sleep over if you want."

"Rrreally?"

"Yes, really."

He grins from ear to ear. Then he looks at me and says, "Get the donnnut. Trust mmme."

* * *

My tires screech as I skid into my parking spot three minutes before the morning bell.

I swear, the crossing guard in front of Aiden's school was fucking with me. He kept me stopped for way longer than necessary. I could've driven all the way to work and back before little Johnny even made it to the crosswalk, but Mr. Tough Guy with his stop sign blocked me for an eternity. I've never wanted to ram my bumper into an eighty-year old man so much in my life.

Aiden's right: I need to get laid.

Too much pent-up testosterone is making me crazy.

Normally I wouldn't sweat about being a few minutes late to work. But I have baked goods to deliver to a certain someone.

The bell rings as I enter the building, and I'm pushing through a sea of kids to get to Michelle's classroom. When I get there, she's bustling around her classroom like a chicken without a head. Dark rings underline her tired eyes.

Something's wrong.

"It's Mr. Hastings!" Joseph shouts from his seat.

Heads snap around, including Michelle's, followed by chairs scraping across the floor as students stand up to run toward me.

"Don't run," Michelle warns. "Guys, stop! Someone's going to get—"

Intense pain shoots through my crotch. I keel over at the waist, dropping the Dunkin Donuts bag and shielding myself from any further harm.

In the midst of their excitement, one of the students knocked me square in the balls.

Michelle raises her voice, ushering students back to their seats. "Give him some space, and get back to your seats!"

Erica, the tiniest student in all of first grade, picks up the trampled brown paper bag. "I'm sorry we squished your donuts, Mr. Hastings."

I take the bag from her and manage to squeak out a "Thank You."

Michelle bites her bottom lip, no doubt to keep from laughing.

Finally able to breathe, I stand and hold out the bag. "Here. I'm sure it tastes just as good in pancake form."

She crosses her arms over her chest. "This wouldn't have happened to you if you would just take *no* as an answer."

I give her my best attempt at puppy dog eyes. "Please, just take it. Don't let the suffering of my balls be for nothing."

She rolls her eyes, but snatches the bag from my grip. "I could care less about your balls. I'm only taking this because I slept through breakfast this morning."

"You look tired."

"Gee, thanks."

"I mean, I can tell that you're tired because you look like you didn't sleep. Wait, that's not what I mean. It's just that your eyes look tired. No, that's not good either ..."

"Please, continue. You're nailing this."

I heave a sigh of defeat. "You look beautiful, Michelle. You always do. But I know you. I can tell when something's wrong."

She drops the crumpled bag onto her desk and shrugs. "I barely got an hour of sleep last night and I'm getting observed by the principal today. I don't feel prepared at all."

"You might not feel prepared, but you are. You'll do great."

She averts her eyes. "Thanks."

"Is that why you didn't sleep?" I know I have no right to ask, but I take a chance anyway.

A wave of sadness flashes across her features before she adjusts her mask. Her wide eyes were always so expressive. I hate it that she feels the need to hide from me.

"Thank you for the donut," she says, defenses locked. "Sorry about your balls."

I wonder what's going on with her as I limp down the hall to the nurse's office. Whatever it is, it has to be important. You don't lose sleep over something trivial.

Is she stressed about work? This job can be stressful.

Is her fiancé treating her right? I have no reason to think otherwise.

Is it her father's health? I really hope not. She adores him.

Is she happy? She deserves to be.

I wish I could be the one she confided in, like she used to.

I wish things between us could be the way they once were.

Nurse Nancy lifts an eyebrow as I hobble into her office. "What'd you do now, Hastings?"

I dig an ice pack out of her freezer and lay it on my junk as I lower myself into a chair. "A kid clipped my family jewels."

She shakes her head. "Always something with you."

Well, at least this solves one of my problems.

Can't get laid if my dick's broken.

4

MICHELLE

"Go get 'em, baby!"

I laugh, shaking my head. "It's a charity game, Dad."

"Dodgeball is dodgeball. Show no mercy ..."

"Take no prisoners," I finish. I send a wink his way before walking onto the court.

The bleachers in the gym are packed with children and their families. I spot several of my students and wave. They jump up and down holding glittery posters, squealing, as if I'm a celebrity.

I really do love this job.

My eyes skate over the crowd. They find their target, and my stomach flip-flops.

Christopher *fucking* Hastings.

He's in a black T-shirt like mine, with our school's name across the front. Red basketball shorts hug his muscular ass, which I am totally not checking out. The backwards baseball hat is the cherry topping off the boyish charm that's oozing from his pores.

There's something about a man in a baseball cap that turns my insides to mush.

Or maybe there's just something about that *man.*

As if he can feel the weight of my stare, Christopher's head turns in my direction. Dimples sink into his cheeks as the grin sprawls across his face. Out of every perfectly formed physical trait on him, my favorite has always been his smile. It's genuine, and it's contagious. He can change your whole mood just by smiling at you. Even now, despite the anger and pain he's caused me, my cheeks twitch, wanting to reciprocate the friendly gesture.

I've heard it takes eleven facial muscles to frown. I'm using all of them right now, fighting the urge to smile back. Just because I accepted his donut doesn't mean we're friends.

You know who *is* my friend though? Karma. She rammed her train right into Christopher's balls the other day. I got a good laugh out of that.

When I reach the center of the gym, Christopher waves me over. "You're on my team, Bambi."

My fists clench at the sound of that nickname on his lips.

Focus, Michelle. Get your head in the game and forget about him.

I decide to survey our team instead. Mrs. Gallagher is a first-grade teacher like me. She's sweet, but she's so old, she looks like she could body double for the Crypt Keeper. I can't for the life of me figure out why she's even playing tonight. Mrs. Stevenson is up there in age too. Those are two of our weakest links. If I was the captain, I'd put them front and center. Get them out of the game before they bust a hip.

We also have our computer teacher, Rebecca. She's uber tall, channeling Sporty Spice with a sweatband around her forehead and loose cargo pants. I don't like to judge people by their appearances, but this could be promising.

Then there's the blond teacher who I caught storming out of the principal's office last week—Christopher called her Raegan. With black streaks under her eyes and a high ponytail, she's shooting daggers with her eyes across the court. I follow her line of sight and land on Principal Waters. *What the hell is going on between those two?*

"Mrs. Gallagher, you and Mrs. Stevenson stay in the back," Christopher begins, rattling off our positions. "Rae and Michelle will stay off to the sides. You ladies are going to distract the other team. Aim low.

"Rebecca and I will be up at the front. They'll be so focused on trying to take us out, Rae and Michelle should be able to pick them off when they're not looking."

I don't tell him that's an easy way to get himself knocked out of the game. In fact, I'm hoping he gets knocked out.

Maybe your ball will "accidentally" slip out of your hand and smack him in the face.

No. That would be bad.

Hilarious, but bad.

We take our spots and the game starts when the whistle blows. I hang back and let my teammates run for the dodgeballs. A good player assesses the opposing team. I don't want to blindly take a shot not knowing who I'm up against.

It doesn't help that Principal Waters is on the opposing team. Hopefully someone knocks him out before I have to. That won't look good for the newbie teacher.

It's a slow start. Seems like everyone's afraid to get into the game. Finally, Christopher throws a ball at Principal Waters, and Rae throws one right after. That second ball whizzes right past his ankle, practically grazing the hairs on his leg, and he looks surprised. It's a good tactic, but it'll only work once. Waters will be watching the two of them like a hawk now.

Instead of retaliating, he launches a ball at Mrs. Stevenson. She makes a decent attempt at catching it, but the ball bounces off her fingers and she's knocked out.

Just like that, we're down one.

Before the whistle screeches at the end of the first round, Rebecca manages to knock two opposing players out of the game and we take the lead. Waters looks pissed. I have a feeling the second round is going to get ugly.

Christopher high-fives each of our teammates. I let him slap my palm, and he winks as he says, "Time to show them what you got."

That wink sends a shiver down my spine.

Damn him.

In the next round, I dodge the balls as they fly by, still the unsuspecting player. Out of the corner of my eye, I catch Christopher nod at Raegan. They're preparing to double-team Principal Waters again.

Not a smart idea.

Before I can get to them, they lob their balls.

Waters effortlessly side-steps one while catching the other.

Christopher's out.

His face is almost as red as his shorts, fists balled at his sides. I do a little happy dance on the inside. Now it's me and Raegan versus our principal and vice principal in the final round.

Raegan smacks my arm playfully. "We got this, new girl."

I smile for the first time since this game started. I've been so wrapped up in my anger with Christopher that I haven't fully enjoyed playing in this game.

It's for charity, for Christ's sake. My students are watching.

Time to give them a show.

The four of us take our places as the whistle cuts through the air. The energy in the room is electric, families shouting and chanting our names. We're each holding onto a ball, waiting for someone to make the first move.

Principal Waters is watching Raegan with a wolfish smirk. Neither he nor Mrs. Wilcox, our VP, are looking at me, which means one of two things: They're complete idiots, or they're planning to fake us out.

I'm prepared for the latter. My guard is up.

At the same time, Waters and Wilcox release their balls, but not at Raegan. They're headed straight for me, fast—one low and one high.

I spring into the air, jumping over the low ball, and stretch my left arm up to catch the high ball, all while cradling my own ball under my right arm.

Deafening screams from the crowd pierce my eardrums. I want to look back to see the look on Christopher's face, but I can't lose concentration. It's two against one. Mrs. Wilcox is out. Somehow, Raegan and I need to take out our principal.

Waters snatches a ball off the floor and stalks to the front of the court. He no longer looks like a boss who's having fun with his employees. He looks like a starving tiger, going in for the kill.

Raegan catches my eye. I shake my head, the slightest movement I can manage. Her eyebrows dip down, and a silent conversation passes between us.

We both lift our arms, ready to throw our balls at Principal Waters. He takes the bait, and raises his ball at the same time. But as our arms come down, we don't let go.

With incredible force, Waters launches his ball at Raegan. It's a little too hard of a throw for a friendly game between coworkers, but Raegan deflects it with her ball, sending his own ball rocketing back at him.

"Yes!" I cry, right before the ball bounces off my principal's face.

Principal Waters tips backward, and collapses onto the floor.

Raegan knocked him out of the game ... literally.

CHRISTOPHER

I rush toward the middle of the gym.

Holy shit. Rae just knocked out our principal.

She's crouched down beside him, while Mrs. Wilcox looks over her shoulder. It's eerily quiet, especially for a room filled with children.

"We need to keep the kids calm," I say to the rest of the teachers.

We each take a section of the gym. I sit beside Aiden on the bottom row of the bleachers, twisting around to talk to some of the students.

"Is he okaaay?" Aiden asks.

"He'll be all right. That ball hit him pretty hard, so he'll probably have a nice shiner tomorrow."

"What's a shiner?" asks Billy, one of the second graders.

"It's a black eye, like a bruise around your eyelid."

Aiden rests his head on my shoulder. "I'm glad yyyou're okay."

Warmth pools in my chest and I smile. "I'm always going to be okay, bud. Don't worry."

I look up to find Michelle's dark eyes on me. On *us*. Confusion draws her eyebrows together. I have no doubt she's wondering who this kid is and why he looks so much like me.

I offer her a small smile, wishing I could answer all of her questions.

I could if she'd let me.

But what would she think? Would she really want to be involved in this life?

Following my line of vision, Aiden asks, "Is that herrr?"

"It is."

"She's rrreally pretty."

"Would you like me to introduce you to her?"

He lifts his head, his eyes searching mine. "If you're nnnot too embarrassed."

My mouth drops open. "Are you kidding me? Why on earth would you say that?"

Cheers fill the room, interrupting Aiden's response. Principal Waters is back on his feet, waving to the crowd. His eye is already starting to swell.

I cup Aiden's chin and say, "We'll finish this conversation later."

Waters takes the microphone and deems Michelle and Raegan the winners of the dodgeball game. After his speech, everyone begins funneling through the gym doors. I hang back with Aiden so he doesn't have to maneuver through the crowd with his crutches.

I spot Raegan talking with Michelle, and I'm glad. Michelle needs a friend here at school, and Rae's one of the nicest humans I've ever met.

"Come on," I say, nudging Aiden with my elbow.

Raegan stops talking when she sees. She throws her arm around Aiden's shoulders. "Hi, handsome. How've you been?"

An adorable blush tinges Aiden's cheeks. "Good."

"Thanks for leaving us out there," she says, turning her attention to me. "Some team captain you are."

I laugh. "You didn't need me. You guys got him good."

She buries her face in her hands. "It was a total accident."

"He threw that ball pretty hard. Waters got what he deserved, if you ask me."

"Do yyyou think you'll get ffffired?" Aiden asks.

"Let's hope not." Rae chuckles and waves. "See you guys tomorrow."

Michelle and I stare at one another, awkward silence descending upon us.

Say something, you moron.

"That wwwas an awesome mmmove," Aiden says, swooping in to save me.

She smiles. "Thanks. I'm Michelle."

I clear my throat, finding my manners. "Michelle, this is, uh … this is Aiden."

Aiden extends his hand, leaning against his crutch for support. "It's nnnice to finally mmmeet you."

Her eyebrows shoot up at his use of the word *finally*. The kid is slick, I'll give him that.

"It's nice to meet you too. How old are you?"

She's trying to do the math, figure out when he was born. It's understandable, given the situation. I just wish I could explain everything.

"I'll be thirrrteen at the end of the mmmonth."

Her head nods slowly, eyes flicking from Aiden to me, and back to Aiden.

"Let's get you home, bud." I clap Aiden on the back. "Do you need a ride?"

Michelle shakes her head. "I came with my dad. He's waiting with the car out front."

"Okay. See you tomorrow then."

"See you tomorrow." Her face brightens as she smiles at Aiden. "It was nice to meet you."

"Yyyou too."

Aiden and I make our way out of the school and into the parking lot. Millions of thoughts swarm my mind, but I have to push them away for now. Aiden's comment weighs on my mind, and I'm eager to get in the car so we can discuss why he's feeling this way.

Once we're buckled and on the road, I glance over at Aiden in the passenger seat. "Why would you think I'd be embarrassed of you?"

He heaves a sigh. "I don't knnnow. Because I'm nnnot like the other kids."

"I know your disability makes you feel different, but that doesn't mean you're something to be embarrassed about."

"You don't undersssstand what it's like." He pauses. "It's mmmore than *feeling* different. I *am* different. I can't rrrun on the playground at rrrecess. I can't play sssports. I can't even sssspeak without sounding like a freak."

Tears brim but I blink them back. This isn't about me. It's about him. "Aiden, maybe the reason you think I'm embarrassed of you is because you're the one who feels embarrassed. You're embarrassed of your disability, and I get it. I'd feel the same way. Hell, I don't have a disability and I've been ashamed to be myself my entire life."

His head turns to look at me. "Rrreally?"

"Yes, really. After my mom passed away, my dad turned into a drunk. He'd show up at school, belligerent and falling down. I was embarrassed to be seen with him because he'd always make a scene wherever we went. And I'm not the most graceful person myself. I'm clumsy and disaster follows me. I never made it on any of the teams I tried out for. Nobody wanted Clumsy Christopher messing everything up."

"Kids called yyyou that?"

I nod. "I know your disability makes you different, but it doesn't have to keep you from having a life. So we're not in the NFL. Big deal. We can find other things that we're good at. You love to read. Maybe you'll be a writer one day, or maybe you'll direct Broadway plays. Who knows? Just don't limit yourself because you have Cerebral Palsy. It limits you enough. Don't limit your own mind."

I stop at the red light in front of us, and look into Aiden's wide eyes. "I could never be embarrassed of you. I'm too proud of you to ever be embarrassed. You're the strongest, most determined person I know. And I love you."

Aiden smiles his lopsided grin. "I love you too."

5

MICHELLE

*W**ho is that boy?*
I'm in the middle of a faculty meeting, and I should be paying attention to what my boss is saying. But all I can think about is Aiden.

He looked an awful lot like Christopher, from their similar skin tones, to the color of their dark features. Thick, unruly hair covered his head, bouncing in his eyes as he took each step toward me. But he'd said he's almost thirteen years old. That would put Christopher at around ten when he was born, making it impossible for Aiden to be his son.

Still, unease twists my gut.

Then there was Aiden's evident disability. He'd needed crutches to walk, but not the kind that tuck under his armpits. They were cuffed to his forearms. His movements were uneven, and his right foot dragged a little.

Despite all that, he wore a sweet smile that pulled to the right. He was absolutely adorable, and my heart swelled when he talked to me with a slight slur elongating his words.

Christopher looked nervous to introduce us. I'm sure I looked nervous too. There are so many questions in need of answering, more now than ever before.

My brother's words ring in my mind: *Maybe the reason he left had nothing to do with you.*

I'm starting to think he's right.

My ears perk up when I hear Mr. Waters announce the need for chaperones for the school's upcoming Halloween dance next month. I've hated Halloween for the past few years. Five, to be exact. The last Halloween party I attended was the one that ended with Christopher in my bed—the first time we made love, and the last night we ever spent together.

But being a teacher means I need to muster all my school spirit for my students. And being the *new* teacher means I have to volunteer to be a chaperone for this dance. So when Principal Waters tells us the sign-up sheet will be in the office, I make a beeline down the hallway.

It's time to leave the past in the past.

Even if I have to face it at work every day.

* * *

MY KNEE BOUNCES UNDER THE TABLE AS I CHECK THE TIME ON MY phone.

My heart sinks when the screen lights up: 6:21PM. Richard said he'd be able to meet me for dinner at five.

Order without him. He's not coming.

He'll be here. He said he would.

Like he's never broken his word to you before?

I glance down at the deliberate cleavage spilling out of my V-neck top. The cleavage I'd hoped would result in me getting some after dinner. Dinner with my fiancé who isn't coming.

The waiter returns to my table for the fourth time. "Any word on your fiancé?"

My cheeks burn but I swallow my pride and shake my head. "Doesn't look like he'll be able to make it. I'll go ahead and order."

"Good for you, hon."

Just as I open my mouth to give the waiter my order, I hear a deep voice behind me say, "Sorry we're late. Traffic was a nightmare."

Christopher and Aiden slide into the booth, both wearing shit-eating grins on their faces.

"Hi, Mmmichelle," Aiden says.

My eyes flick between the charming duo. "What are you guys doing?"

"Eating dinner, silly. We got held up at the doctor's office," Christopher says.

"His phonnne died, so we couldn't call yyyou."

My eyes narrow, shooting Christopher a look that reads: *You're making the kid lie for you now?*

Christopher's eyes sparkle with amusement.

The waiter fans himself with a menu as he places his hand on my shoulder. "Honey, he's worth the wait."

I cross my arms over my chest. "What if he made you wait five years? Would you still have waited?"

Christopher's eyes never leave mine. "You're not the only one who's been waiting."

Our gazes sear into each other, filling the space between us with electricity.

"Why don't I give you boys some time to look over the menu?" the waiter asks.

"That would be great. Thank you."

"No problem." The waiter leans toward me and whispers, "And I'll go grab you a knife so you can cut through all that tension."

A clueless Aiden slaps his menu on the table. "I'm getting a cheeseburrrger."

"What the hell are you guys doing here?" I ask.

Christopher jerks his thumb in Aiden's direction. "It was his idea."

"Blame the kid. Real nice."

"We came to grab a bite to eat, and saw you sitting here."

"You looked like yyyou were sad," Aiden says. "I didn't wwwant you to eat alonnne."

I shake my head, fighting the smile that's tugging on my lips.

"If you really want us to go, just say the word. I don't want to make you uncomfortable," Christopher says.

I heave a sigh and the stress rolls back out to sea. "No, stay. I don't mind the company."

"Yyyou look pretty."

"Thanks, Aiden. You're very sweet."

Christopher's heated stare tells me he agrees, but he says nothing to confirm it.

"So, are you feeling okay?" I ask. "Why were you at the doctor's?"

"I go to the doctor's all the timmme. I get check-ups and physical therrrapy."

"Can I ask ... what do you ... what's wrong?"

"Cerrrebral Palsy."

I nod, taking a long sip of my water. I'd Googled Aiden's symptoms the night after the dodgeball game, and that was one of the options I'd come across. *A condition marked by impaired muscle coordination, typically caused by damage to the brain before or at birth*, the New Oxford American Dictionary had said. I don't know much about CP, except that people can have varying degrees of severity. There were pictures of kids in wheelchairs, and I wondered if Aiden was in one when he was younger. The way he looks now, you'd almost never notice he has a disability.

"My mmmom's a drrrug addict," Aiden says matter-of-factly.

"Aiden!" Christopher scolds.

"What? It's the trrruth."

I smile. "I like your bluntness. The painful truth is always better than a sugarcoated lie."

"My mmmom dropped me off at mmmy grandfather's house wwwhen I was eight. I haven't seen her since."

When I was eight. That means ...

Realization sets in, hitting me like a wave. It knocks me down and sends me tumbling under the freezing water. My vision blurs and I can't see straight. I hear voices around me but they're muffled.

I'm pulled under and sink to the bottom of the ocean, alone with my thoughts.

Five years ago, Christopher left. He dropped out of school and left everything behind. He left *me* behind. We fell in love and everything was perfect. Then he was gone. All this time, I couldn't imagine what was so important, what made him drop everything and run.

Aiden. It was Aiden.

Christopher had mentioned his broken family—alcoholic father, junkie sister—but I never delved into the details. It was a sore subject for him. The only one he'd ever willingly talk about was his mom.

I didn't know he had a nephew.

More information I'd read about Cerebral Palsy on Google pops into my mind: Cerebral Palsy can be caused by substance abuse.

Christopher's sister used while she was pregnant, giving this debilitating disorder to an innocent baby, and then abandoned him. How did she survive nine years before that? God only knows the things Aiden must've seen at such a young age.

The missing pieces of the puzzle snap into place. All except one. I still don't know why Christopher didn't tell me he was leaving. And that's the part that hurt most of all.

I jump at the touch of a hand on my shoulder. "Hon, are you ready to order?"

I blink up at the waiter.

"We're ready," Christopher says. "We'll take three cheeseburgers, well done. No pickles, please."

"You got it, handsome." He spins on his heels and waltzes away from us.

"Are yyyou okay, Michelle?"

I gulp my water until half the glass is empty. Then I force my mouth into a smile. "Yeah, sorry. I was just surprised to hear about your mom."

Aiden nods like he understands. "Uncle Chris says drugs make people crazy, so Mom wasn't able to think straight when she left me."

My chest aches. For Aiden. For his mother.

And for Christopher.

He's not making eye-contact with me now. I want to reach across the table and smooth out the worry lines between his eyebrows with my thumb, like I used to. I want to wrap my arms around him and tell him how sorry I am about what he's had to endure.

Most of all, I want to tell him how proud I am. Proud of him for putting his family first, for raising a child when he was still a kid himself, for being the amazing person he is.

I swallow the emotion lodged in my throat. "You're lucky to have an uncle like Christopher."

Aiden nudges him with his shoulder. "Yyyeah. I guess he's okay."

Christopher smiles, but it doesn't reach his eyes.

"So, wwwhy were yyyou sitting here alone?" Aiden asks.

I'd already forgotten all about Richard standing me up. "My fiancé was supposed to meet me for dinner, but he got held up at work."

"Wwwhere does he work?"

"He's a lawyer."

"They mmmake a lot of mmmoney."

"Aiden, Jesus." Christopher runs a hand through his hair. "You can't say things like that."

"It's okay, really," I say laughing. "You're right, Aiden. They do make a lot of money. But they also miss out on spending time with their loved ones."

"Is that why yyyou looked so sad? Because he's spending time at work and nnnot with yyyou?"

"It's complicated," is all I say.

"That's what adults say wwwhen they think I wwwon't understand something."

My smile widens. "I think you understand a lot. You're very perceptive." My eyes flick to Christopher. "Just like your uncle."

Our burgers arrive, and Christopher remains quiet while we eat.

Aiden does most of the talking, and I don't mind. It's easy to forget he's only twelve.

"When's your birthday?" I ask him, after the waiter hands us dessert menus.

"Halloween."

"That's soon. Are you having a party?"

He shakes his head. "Uncle Chris said he'd take mmme and my best friend to the arrrcade that wwweekend. I don't have enough frrriends for a party."

My chest squeezes. "Well, now you have two friends." I point my index finger at myself.

Aiden's face lights up. "Wwwill yyyou come to the arcade?"

Before I can answer, someone standing beside our table catches my attention.

Richard.

CHRISTOPHER

As if this dinner couldn't get more awkward.

Richard's cold blue eyes roam around the table before settling back on Michelle. "I got held up at work."

No apology. No remorse. Just a robotic statement. I can tell the guy's a dick before he breathes another word.

Michelle's back is ramrod straight, doe eyes wide. "I didn't think you were coming, since I didn't hear from you. My friends saw me sitting alone, so they joined me for dinner."

"Friends," Richard says, narrowing his eyes as he looks back at me and then Aiden. He extends his hand. "Richard Deveraux."

Only a douchebag tells you his last name when he introduces himself. *You're not James Bond, dude. Stop it.*

I give his hand a firm shake. "Chris, and this is Aiden."

I'd say it's nice to meet him, but it's not.

"Thank you for keeping my fiancé company while she waits." He slips his leather wallet out of his pocket and sifts through his cash before dropping a hundred-dollar bill onto the table. "This should cover it."

He might as well have unzipped his fly and dropped his hammer cock onto the table.

He could've taken out other bills. I'm sure he has twenties in there. Maybe a few tens. But he chose the Benjamin Franklin to make a statement. Another dick move.

"That's not necessary," I say, handing the crisp bill back to him.

Ignoring me, Richard holds his hand out for Michelle. "Let's go home, babe."

Babe. My stomach churns and I fear my burger is going to make a reappearance. *Babe* is such a generic nickname. The guy clearly has no creativity. I wonder if he knows that her mother used to call her Bambi. If he knows anything about her mother at all.

What the hell does Michelle see in this guy?

To my surprise, Michelle remains seated. "I'll meet you there. We were about to order dessert."

Richard says nothing. He just stares down at her, his head tilted to one side. His expression reads: *Well, look at you.*

I want to knock it off his face.

I don't realize my fists are clenched until I feel Aiden nudge me with his knee under the table.

Michelle turns her attention back to Aiden, though Dickface is still standing beside her. "I'm sorry, Aiden. What were you saying?"

I can't hide my smug smile while the two talk about Skee-ball and air hockey, and Richard makes his exit.

We order dessert, and I insist on paying when the check comes. "You can give Dick his money back."

Michelle's eyebrows furrow. "Don't call him that."

"I call it like I see it." I shrug. "You used to do the same."

"Well, you know what? I'd rather a dick than a coward." She stuffs the hundred into her purse and scoots out of the booth.

Aiden's blocking me in, and I contemplate shoving him onto the floor so I can run after her.

Aiden just shakes his head. "Yyyou pissed herrr off."

"Come on, the guy's a dick."

"She knows that. But yyyou're the one she's mmmad at."

"And he's the one she's going home to."

"Should've taken his mmmoney."

6

MICHELLE

The tick of the clock gets louder with each passing minute.

I have to take my class to gym, but I don't want to see Christopher. Mondays have officially become my most-hated day of the week.

They don't need gym, right? It's not like children require physical activity or anything. I could put on some *Descendants* songs and they'd be just as happy dancing around the classroom.

"What do you guys say we skip gym and just have a dance party here instead?"

I'm all but stoned to death as the kids jeer and groan.

My shoulders slump. "Fine, line up."

We walk down the hall and wait outside the gym door. Emily, my line leader for the week, smiles up at me. "I love gym. Mr. Hastings is the best. He lets us play fun games and he's super nice."

I thought so too, kid

I offer her a genuine smile in return. I can't let my disdain for her beloved gym teacher dull her excitement. "I used to love gym when I was in school too."

"That's because you were good at it," Christopher says. He leans against the doorframe of the gym, arms crossed over his chest, putting his biceps on display. "Miss Figueroa is an athletic freak of nature."

Emily giggles. "I bet you were really good in gym too, Mr. Hastings."

He shakes his head. "I wasn't. I was the dorky kid with glasses and two left feet."

Her eyes widen. "Two left feet?" She looks down at his neon green Nike sneakers.

Christopher chuckles. "It's just an expression. It means I was clumsy."

"Still is," I say under my breath.

He gestures for the class to enter the gym, giving a fist-bump to each student as they step inside. They beam up at him, as if he's a superhero. I suppose to them he is.

I once looked at him the same way.

"Excuse me." Gary rolls a large garbage can on wheels into the gym, disappearing inside Christopher's office.

Christopher steps to the side and then turns back to me. "I forgot to thank you. Gary and I are going on our first date this week. So kind of you to set us up the way you did."

I stifle a laugh, recalling Gary's confused expression when I'd told him Christopher wanted his number. "Glad I could be of service."

The last student on my line stops in front of us. "You're going on a date with Mr. Gary?" Isaiah asks, looking up at Christopher with a scrunched-up nose.

Christopher opens his mouth, but I cut him off. "He is. Isn't that sweet?"

Isaiah shakes his head. "My mom's gonna be mad. I heard her talking to Anthony's mom during Back to School Night. She said you're a stud muffin." He shrugs. "Whatever that means."

I turn my face away to conceal my laughter until Isaiah takes his spot on the floor inside the gym.

Christopher's cheeks are bright red. "Great. Isaiah's mom is the PTO president. The entire school will think I'm gay by tomorrow."

"It's good for the kids to be exposed to that sort of thing. Creates an inclusive environment."

He smirks as he leans in. "I've really missed your spunk."

Goosebumps spread like wildfire across my skin, the familiar scent of Irish Spring soap flooding my senses. I roll my eyes, attempting to appear unaffected by his proximity.

You are so affected.

I'm walking away when Christopher calls after me. "Now that you know the truth, I hope you can understand why I had to leave you."

"I do," I say over my shoulder. "But it doesn't make things between us any different."

With that, I turn and make my way back down the hall.

* * *

"THERE SHE IS!"

Mrs. Gallagher lifts her hand so slowly, I'm not sure if she's trying to wave at me or hail a cab. "It's about damn time you showed up for lunch."

"I'm sorry," I say, taking the seat beside her. She might be old, but she's the only friend I've got at school right now. The other ladies in my grade level aren't very welcoming, and they keep to themselves. "I work through lunch most days."

"That's how it is for new teachers. You'll settle in soon."

I nod as I unwrap my tuna sandwich and take a huge bite.

By lunchtime, teachers are so hungry that the faculty room transforms into an episode of Planet Earth—the scene when the music takes a dramatic turn, and the predatory cat finally catches up to the elusive prey, sinking its teeth into the helpless animal. We scarf our food down our throats and pray we won't have to poop for the remaining three hours without a break in our day.

I scan the room, scoping out the teachers in attendance. Christopher doesn't have the same lunch period as me. Sadly, neither does Raegan. She and I connected at the dodgeball game, and I've been hoping to run into her again.

Several of the second-grade teachers are sitting around the table next to us talking about their students:

"The kid just doesn't listen!"

"Is he the one with the spikey blond hair?"

"No, his hair is brown. Same color as the shit he smeared all over the boy's bathroom."

"I can't imagine getting that phone call as a mother."

Mrs. Gallagher speaks up. "You should send him to Hastings. I had a student like that last year and Chris set him straight. He got to go play in the gym as a reward for good behavior."

A surprising sense of pride swells in my chest upon hearing how great Christopher is with the kids here. He's making a difference in their lives, which is all a teacher could hope for.

One of the teachers winks. "I wish I could go to Mr. Hastings for good behavior."

"Back off," another woman chimes in. "If anyone's getting with Chris, it's me."

The idea of seeing him with someone else sours my stomach. I hadn't even thought about that until now.

Shouldn't matter. You're with Dick, remember?

A third teacher waves her hand. "You two can fight over the boy. I'll take Principal Waters. That man is fine with a capital F."

Cheers and claps fill the room in agreement.

Mrs. Gallagher shakes her head and leans in so only I can hear. "Nothing hornier than a school full of female teachers."

I giggle. "The two men in question are quite handsome. Can't say I blame them."

"And how about your man?" she asks. "What does he look like?"

I press the home button on my phone, illuminating the screen: A picture of Richard with his arm around me at his firm's Christmas party last year.

Mrs. Gallagher smiles. "He's handsome. You two will make beautiful babies."

"Thank you." My lips pull downward, recalling the conversation we'd had the other night.

I've always wanted kids, but I don't want to raise them alone while my husband works. I want it to be a joint effort. I just don't know if Richard is capable of putting work behind his family.

He hasn't been able to do it for you. What makes you think he'll do it for a baby?

Babies can change people.

Do you think he could do what Christopher did with Aiden?

"When's the wedding, Michelle?" Rebecca asks.

"We haven't set a date yet."

Her eyebrows perk up. "How long have you been engaged for?"

"Six months."

"Have you gone dress shopping?" Mrs. Gallagher asks. "That's always fun."

I shake my head. "No."

"My mom was more of a bridezilla than I was," Rebecca says. "Whatever you do, don't let your mother pressure you into buying a dress you don't love. If it were up to her, I would've looked like the Stay Puft Marshmallow Man."

People don't realize how much they take for granted in life. Trivial things to some are significant to others. Having a mother who nags you might be irritating, but there's someone out there wishing she had a mother to nag her.

Like me. I wish my mother was here to go dress shopping with.

Tears prick my eyes.

Not again.

Pushing out of my chair, I stand and grab my things. "I just remembered I have to call a parent. Have a good afternoon."

I rush out of the faculty room and make my way to my classroom as quickly as I can.

* * *

"You're quiet tonight."

"Hmm?"

Richard slips the book out of my hands and places it face-down on the bed. "Everything okay?"

Looking into his pale-blue eyes, I force a smile. "Fine. Why?"

"You've barely said two words since I got home."

"It's been a long day. Guess I'm just tired."

His eyebrow arches. "Wanna try that again with the truth, this time?"

I shake my head, and look up at the ceiling. "A girl at work was talking about how her mother helped her pick out her wedding dress, and I guess ... I don't know. When we got engaged, I had my family to share it with. But my dad and my brothers can't come dress shopping with me. I guess it's the first time in a long time that I feel like I really need my mom here."

"Ah. I see." He wraps his arm around my shoulders and pulls me to his chest.

I relax against the warmth of his body and close my eyes, listening to the steady beat of his heart.

"Maybe you should go dress shopping this weekend. Get it over with so it's not looming over you. I can ask my mom to go with you, if you'd like."

He's totally missing the point.

He's just trying to help.

"I don't think I'm ready for that yet." I chew the inside of my cheek as I mull over my thoughts. "Maybe we can talk about setting a date though."

"I thought we agreed on taking our time with that?"

I crane my neck to look up at him. "We did, but there's no harm in setting a date. At least then we'd have a timeframe."

"I'm trying to make partner at the firm. They'll be announcing their pick sometime next year. If I make it, taking time off for a wedding and a honeymoon won't look good."

All about work. Par for the course.

"Okay." I slide out from under his arm and scoot back over to my side of the bed, bringing my book with me.

"You're mad."

I shake my head. "I'm not. I get it. Work has to come first right now."

Will it always?

"Thank you for being so understanding." Richard leans over and I let him peck my lips. "I love you."

A small, jagged fragment of my heart breaks off, floating away with our conversation.

"I love you too."

7

MICHELLE

"I'm not wearing that."

Raegan's bottom lip juts out as she returns the costume to the shelf. "You're no fun."

"We work in a school. We can't wear half of these costumes to the Halloween dance."

"Well, maybe not this one." She points to a Playboy Bunny costume, which is basically a onesie with ears. "But we can still look cute!"

My eyes land on the super hero section. "What about those?"

Raegan scrunches her nose.

I sigh. "If you can find something that doesn't scream, *I'm a street walker,* then I'll buy it. Just hurry up. I'm starving."

"Didn't you just eat before you met me here?"

I cross my arms over my chest. "You know what? I don't really like your tone."

She giggles and drapes her arm over my shoulders. "Hey, no judgement. I used to eat like you when I was in my twenties."

"You say it like you're so much older than me. I thought thirty was the new twenty, or some shit like that."

She grimaces. "Don't remind me. I wasted an entire decade that I'll never get back!"

My eyebrows press together. "What do you mean?"

"I was married for most of my twenties. Turns out, he was the wrong guy. Now I'm single. At thirty. I can't even fathom the idea of dating someone again. The rules are all different, and I don't even want to play the damn game."

I nod. "If I didn't meet Richard at a bar, I don't know where I'd go to meet someone. Online dating is just scary."

"That might be my only option," she murmurs. "Come on. Let's check in this aisle."

As we turn the corner, I spot Christopher and Aiden across the store. Without thinking, I grab Raegan's arm and yank her behind a shelf.

"Get down!" I whisper.

"Why are we getting down? Who's there?"

That's when I realize how odd this looks. She has no idea who Christopher is to me, or that we even know each other prior to working together.

Plus, there's the small fact of you being with Richard.

Yeah, that too. I need to come up with an excuse. "Christopher and Aiden are over there. We should sneak up on them and scare them."

Raegan's eyes dart around until she spots the mask section. "Genius! Let's go."

We look like complete morons creeping around the store, waddling with our knees bent and our heads down, giggling the entire way. Raegan chooses the classic *Scream* mask, while I go for the werewolf head. Then we edge closer to where Christopher and Aiden are standing with their backs to us.

I hold up my fingers for a three-count, and then we jump out from behind the shelf, screaming and lunging toward the boys.

Aiden jumps and quickly recovers.

But Christopher ...

Oh, Christopher.

He flies backward, clutching his chest, and smacks into the shelf.

One of the metal brackets snaps off, and everything on the shelf dumps onto the floor. Several customers pop their heads into our aisle to see what all the commotion is about.

Raegan and I rip our masks off, laughing so hard we can't breathe.

Aiden's laughing too. "Yyyou guys got us good."

Raegan gasps for air. "That. Was. Amazing."

Christopher's chest heaves up and down. "I think I just shit myself!"

"Let's hope not." I pull Aiden into a hug. "Sorry for scaring you. I saw you guys standing here and I just couldn't help myself."

Aiden grins. "Wwwe're going to get yyyou back."

"Bring it!"

Christopher shakes his head. "I wouldn't mess with her, bud. She grew up with three brothers. This girl is the prank queen."

Raegan lifts her eyebrows. "Do you guys know each other?"

"Michelle and I used to—"

"We had the same class together in college," I say, cutting off whatever Christopher was about to delve into. "Small world."

"Really small." Raegan's eyes bounce between us. She doesn't believe me for a second, but hopefully she lets it go. I don't feel like rehashing all the gory details about what happened between us.

"Wwwhat are yyyou going to be for Halloween?" Aiden asks.

"Not sure yet. We're still browsing." I jerk my thumb toward Raegan. "If this one can find an outfit that covers more of my body parts than it shows."

She shrugs. "It's not my fault Halloween is a skanky holiday."

Christopher's eyes flick to mine, a wistful gleam reflecting in them. "I was never a big fan of Halloween. Not until a few years ago."

"What happened? You get laid or something?" Raegan jokes.

His gaze doesn't waver from mine. "Yeah, something like that."

My stomach churns at the reminder of the unforgettable night we shared. No matter what I do, no matter how much I've blocked him from my mind all these years, that one memory never fades.

The way he looked at me when I undressed before him, like he'd never seen anyone more beautiful in his life; the way he touched me, like I was the most precious thing to behold; the way he made love to me, like we'd be together forever ... it was the single most romantic, sensual, magical night of my life.

Sometimes, after Richard and I have sex, I think about that night with Christopher. Then I remember how it felt waking up without him the next morning, and my sex life suddenly doesn't seem so bad. Richard might lack passion, but he's in that bed every morning when I get up. That has to count for something.

I roll my eyes. "Halloween is overrated." Then I hook my arm around Raegan's elbow. "Back to costume shopping. Bye, boys."

"Okay, I'm gonna need you to tell me everything," Raegan says, once we're out of earshot.

"Nothing to tell. Oh, look. How about that costume?"

She gives me a blank stare. "I am not going to dress up as a nun for Halloween. Now tell me what happened between you two."

"Fine." I cross my arms over my chest and narrow my eyes. "I'll tell you anything you want to know, as long as you tell me what's going on between you and our boss."

Her mouth falls open before she can catch it. "I, uh, I have no idea what you're talking about. Now let's concentrate on finding an outfit."

"Uh-huh. That's what I thought."

We scour the shelves until we decide on matching witch costumes. The dress is girly enough for Raegan, and long enough to cover the length of my thighs. We pay and make our way to the food court after.

"So what does Richard look like?" Raegan asks, taking a bite of her pizza.

I slide my phone across the table.

Her green eyes light up as she pulls the screen closer. "He's a hottie! Good for you, girl."

I chuckle. "He is nice to look at."

"Light eyes, light hair. He's the exact opposite of Chris."

I shrug, taking my phone back. "I don't have a type."

"Oh, I totally have a type. Tall, dark, and handsome. Gets me every time."

"Like our principal," I say, arching an eyebrow.

"Isn't Aiden adorable?"

I smirk at the blatant change of subject. "He is."

"I can't imagine what he must feel, knowing his own mother abandoned him." She shakes her head. "That has to mess with your head."

"He seems like he's doing okay, given the circumstances."

"He's an old man inside a kid's body."

I laugh. "He really is."

"Crazy how Christopher gave up everything for him. He was only nineteen. His life could've turned out very different had he not left college to take care of his nephew." She eyes me over the rim of her cup.

I nod, averting my eyes. "Yeah."

"Oh, come on!" She smacks the table with her palm. "You're not going to give me anything?"

"Nope."

"Next time we go out, I'm getting you drunk."

8

CHRISTOPHER

"Wwwow. This place looks innncredible."

"Michelle and Rae did most of the work," I say.

"Yeah," Raegan says, laughing. "Your uncle helped by eating half the bowl of cheese balls while we put up all the Halloween decorations."

Aiden shakes his head. "Sounds about rrright."

"No one knows how you stay in such good shape when you eat like a garbage disposal. Must be nice to be a man."

Out of the corner of my eye, I catch Michelle enter through the cafeteria doors. My attention is drawn to her. In black ankle boots, purple and black striped knee-high stockings, a black corset dress with purple laces, and a wide-brimmed witch hat, she's the perfect combination of sexy and sweet.

The first thing to pop into my mind is bending her over in that dress.

The next is the fact that she'll be going home to her fiancé in that dress.

My stomach rolls.

"She's engaged, you know," Raegan whispers.

"I'm well-aware." I fix my forlorn expression and look at Rae, who's in the same costume as Michelle. "Was there a buy one/get one on witch costumes?"

She jabs me in the stomach. "Don't hate. We look cute. Oh, no. Tommy! No boogers in the punch." She groans. "I'll be back."

"Where's she running off to?" Michelle asks as she approaches.

"Booger duty."

She scrunches her adorable nose. "I don't even want to know."

"Just donnn't drink the punnnch," Aiden says.

"Noted. So, are you excited for your birthday tomorrow?"

"I can't wwwait to school Uncle Chris in air hockey."

"To be fair, it's not that hard to school your uncle."

"Hey," I say, feigning offense.

Aiden chuckles. "I like yyyour costume, Mmmichelle."

"Thanks. You look great. I would've made a Bucky costume if I'd have known. Every Cap' needs a Bucky."

Aiden's eyes widen. "That wwwould've been awesommme."

I splurged on Aiden's Captain America costume, so I wasn't able to spend unnecessary money on myself. Instead, I threw on a football jersey and smudged black lines under my eyes. Not too original, but it's cost-effective.

Michelle turns her attention to me. "Really thought you were gonna be dressed up as a ghost."

My eyebrows dip down. "Really? Why?"

She shrugs. "You're so good at ghosting people. Would've been fitting." She pops a cheeseball into her mouth and struts away.

As much as I hate the way she continues to throw my transgression in my face every chance she gets, I grin.

She wouldn't harbor this much anger towards me if she didn't still care about me. That has to count for something.

Right?

When I saw she'd signed up to be a chaperone at tonight's Halloween dance, I begged Aiden to come with me.

"What's in it for mmme?" he'd asked.

Little con artist. I'm not comfortable leaving him home alone yet, so I bribed him with fifty bucks and a red slushy from 7-Eleven.

The slushy killed me more than the money did. He was on a sugar high for two hours last night.

Is it wrong to use a child to my advantage? Yes.

Did I go through with it anyway? Also yes.

It's worth it just watching the way Aiden lights up whenever he's with Michelle.

I get it, buddy.

She talks to him like he's an adult, and he eats that shit up. I'm actually learning a lot from watching her interactions with him.

"Uncle Chris?"

"Yeah, bud?"

"Michelle's cool."

"I know."

"Donnn't let her mmmarry Dick."

I rest a hand on Aiden's shoulder. "If only it were that easy."

* * *

MICHELLE SPENDS THE MAJORITY OF THE PARTY BY RAEGAN'S SIDE. I give her space, though my heart is straining against my chest.

"I'm gonna head to the bathroom, bud. Need to go?"

Aiden shakes his head. "Nnno. I'll stay here and mmmake sure Tommy doesn't flick his boogers into the punnnch again."

Out in the hallway, I round the corner and smack right into Michelle. The contents of her purse spill onto the floor.

"I'm so sorry," I say.

"It's okay." She kneels down to collect her things.

I bend down to help, and a loud ripping sound echoes in the empty hallway.

Shit.

Both of our eyes go wide.

"Was that ..."

"It was," I say, confirming that my pants definitely did just split open.

Her lips twitch. "Do you have an extra pair of pants handy?"

"Nope."

"Let me see how bad the tear is."

I stand with both of my hands clutching my backside. "No."

"Come on, turn around. Maybe we can staple it."

A student exits the boy's bathroom. "Hey, Mr. Hastings." He eyes me suspiciously. "What are you doing?"

"I, uh ..."

"Mr. Hastings had a bit of an accident, Ryan."

I shoot Michelle a death glare.

She grins.

Ryan nods like he understands. "I had an accident in pre-school once. The kids called me poopy pants for the rest of the year."

"Oh, no, I didn't poop my pants, Ryan."

"It's okay, Mr. Hastings. Your secret is safe with me." Ryan zips his lips and heads back into the cafeteria.

Perfect.

A laugh bursts from Michelle's throat.

"First I'm gay. Next I poop my pants." I shake my head. "Any more rumors you'd like to spread about me?"

"Oh, I've got an entire school year of possibilities."

"I'm terrified and excited at the same time."

She giggles. "Come on, poopy pants. I've got a stapler in my classroom."

I slide along the perimeter of the hallway until we're in the safety of her classroom. I flick on the lights and Michelle sinks into her chair, stapler in hand.

"You *are* wearing underwear, correct?"

I choke out a laugh. "Yes, of course. One doesn't go commando in a school building."

"All right. Turn around."

"You're not going to staple my pants to my ass, are you?"

"The thought did cross my mind."

My body stiffens. "Michelle ..."

"I'm kidding, I'm kidding. Relax."

I reluctantly shuffle in a circle.

"Are you seriously wearing Superman boxer-briefs?"

My cheeks burn. Forgot I had these on. "Yes. Yes, I am."

"You do realize you're twenty-four, right?"

I twist to look at her over my shoulder. "A man is never too old for Superman."

She starts to smile but catches herself, and clears her throat. "It's ripped right along the seam. I can staple it but you're not going to be able to sit for the rest of the night."

"That's fine. We've got an hour left."

She pinches the material together and I hear the click of the stapler.

"Can I ask you a question?"

"Anything," I say.

Please. Ask me whatever's going on in that beautiful head of yours.

"Where's your sister?"

I heave a sigh. "I don't know. She disappeared when she left Aiden with my dad."

"Does Aiden ever ask about her?"

"No. Part of me wishes he would. I never know what he's thinking."

"Maybe it's too painful for him to talk about."

"Talking about it can make you feel better." I eye Michelle over my shoulder again. "He reminds me a lot of you in that regard."

She looks away, putting surgeon-like focus on the stapler.

I want to keep her talking. So I ask a question that's been on my mind since the first day I saw her here, even though it's the last thing I want to talk about. "When's the wedding?"

"Please don't, Christopher."

"Don't what?"

"Don't pretend like you care about my wedding."

"I care about *you.*"

"Clearly. That's why you called my fiancé a dick at dinner the other night, right?"

When I spin around to face her, she stands and tries to push past me.

I catch her wrist and tug her back in front of me. "Look, I'm sorry for upsetting you. But I won't apologize for what I said about him. It's the truth. And you're mad because you know it too."

She presses her lips into a firm line, eyes blazing up at me. "Just add it to the list of apologies you owe me."

Before I can think better of it, I caress her cheek with the back of my hand. She doesn't lean into my touch, like she used to, but she doesn't pull away either.

That's progress.

"I still can't believe that you're here," I whisper. "Right in front of me. It's like a dream."

There's so much more I want to say, so much unfinished business between us. It's in this moment that I realize Aiden's right: I had her first.

Fate has thrown us back together, and I won't believe that it's sheer happenstance. Michelle holds my heart in her hands. I belong to her. I can't let her marry someone else. I can't give up on us. Not yet.

Not without a fight.

"I know you need time. Time to adjust to me being back in your life. Time to forgive me for what I did. And that's okay." I cup her face and draw her closer to me. "Because this time around, I'm not going anywhere."

Her chest rises and falls rapidly. "Is that supposed to be a threat?"

"No. It's a promise. And I'm going to prove it to you."

"Don't waste your time."

"Time is all I've got."

I feel her body shiver, and for a split second, her eyes fall to my lips. But before she can say anything more, the classroom door opens and rips us out of this important moment.

Raegan's standing in the doorway, eyes bouncing between us. "Hey, guys. We should start cleaning up soon. Most of the kids have started to leave."

Michelle drops the stapler onto her desk and walks away from me without so much as a look back in my direction.

9

MICHELLE

I lay my dirty plate into the sink with a sigh.

Another dinner alone.

Better get used to it if you're going to marry Dick.

In the living room, I flop onto the couch and prop my feet up onto the coffee table. I channel surf, looking for a good movie to get lost in. Nothing romantic. Nothing pertaining to love at all.

Not after the intense moment in my classroom with Christopher last night.

I'd be lying if I said it didn't feel incredible to be that close to him again. To have him looking down at me with a mixture of love and lust in his eyes. To feel like everything was as perfect as it was five years ago.

So I'm just not going to say anything at all.

My phone buzzes on the armrest beside me and I jump. My heartrate speeds up even more when I see Christopher's name on the screen.

For years, I'd prayed for him to call me. Prayed to see his name pop up on my phone. Now here we are, and it's not at all how I'd imagine it would be.

That's life, I guess. Nothing ever goes the way you think it will.

"Hello?"

"Michelle, hi. It's Chris."

"I know. What's going on?"

I hear him blow out a shaky breath. "I'm sorry to bother you. But I don't know what else to do."

My stomach twists at the desperation in his voice. Something's wrong, otherwise he wouldn't be calling. "Is Aiden okay?"

"His best friend cancelled on the arcade for his birthday tonight. He's home with a stomach bug."

"Oh, no. Aiden was so excited to go."

"Yeah, well, I told him we could still go, just the two of us ... but he won't come out of his room."

I'm silent for a moment. The poor kid only has one friend, and now he has to spend his birthday alone. Guilt gnaws at me.

Glancing at the time on the cable box, I stand. "Text me your address."

* * *

My GPS TAKES ME ABOUT FIFTEEN MINUTES AWAY, INTO A SHITTY part of town.

How did a boy from the south end up in New Jersey anyway?

Just add that to my mountain of questions.

When I pull into a parking spot, Christopher's sitting on the steps outside his apartment.

"He still in his room?" I ask, walking up the path.

"Yup. I didn't tell him you were coming." He stands, running his fingers through his hair. "Thank you."

I slip my hands into my back pockets. "I couldn't let him stay locked in his room on his birthday."

Instead of turning to go inside, Christopher remains where he is.

"Well, are we gonna go inside, or does Aiden sleep out here somewhere?"

There's so much emotion in his eyes as he holds my stare. Worry.

Fear. Frustration. "Look, this apartment is all I can afford right now. But I'm saving up to buy something nicer for us one day."

"You don't have to explain your situation. Do you really think I'd judge you for where you live?"

He lifts a shoulder and lets it fall. "You're marrying a lawyer. You must be living a very different life now."

I'm instantly angered by his statement, but I'm not here to argue. I'm here for Aiden. "Just show me where his room is."

My eyes dart around as we step inside. The apartment is definitely small. The kitchen, dining room, and living room are all in one open space. The countertops and appliances are outdated, and there's yellowed stains on the walls. The living room consists of a couch, a recliner, and an old television set.

My brothers would have a conniption if they had to watch Sunday football games on that screen.

None of those things matter, though. As long as a home is filled with love, it doesn't matter what it looks like. But the one thing I'm worried by is the fact that there aren't pictures hanging up anywhere. No personal touches or decorations of any kind.

What does Aiden think of this place?

Christopher leads me into the narrow hallway and gestures to the first door on my left.

I knock lightly. "Aiden? It's Michelle. Can I come in?"

After a few seconds of silence, Christopher shakes his head. Then, the door cracks open.

I shoot him a triumphant look before disappearing inside Aiden's room.

"Hey. What's going on?"

Aiden lowers himself onto the edge of his bed, leaning his crutches against his nightstand. "Jordan's sick. He can't commme to the arrrcade."

I sit beside him, and the mattress squeaks under my weight. "I'm sorry. That really sucks."

He nods, staring down at the stained carpet.

"You can still go, you know."

He shakes his head. "It's nnno fun playing those games by mmmyself."

"Who says anything about playing by yourself?" I nudge him with my shoulder. "I'm down for some air hockey."

His big hazel eyes meet mine. "Yyyou don't have to do that. Yyyou wouldn't be here if Jorrrdan hadn't cancelled."

"And neither would you. But Jordan cancelled, and now I'm here because that's what friends are for. They're always there for you when you need them."

"Whaddya say, bud?" Christopher's leaning against the door-frame, watching us.

I hold up my fist. "Until the end of the line, Cap'."

A crooked smile creeps onto Aiden's face. "Let's go, Bucky."

* * *

THE NEXT TWO HOURS ARE SPENT SCHOOLING THE BOYS IN EVERY game on the boardwalk while eating our weight in cotton candy.

"I wwwant to play that one nnnext." Aiden points to the water gun game where you have to aim the water into the clown's mouth until the balloon pops.

I pat Christopher on his shoulder. "You might want to sit this one out. This requires aim."

He scoffs. "Hey, I can aim just fine."

Aiden grins. "Tell that to ourrr toilet seat."

My head falls back as I laugh. I give Aiden a fist-bump and take a seat on the stool between them.

"Oh, it's on now," Christopher says.

When the bell sounds, our balloons start to swell. It looks like I'm in the lead, but I won't take my eyes off the bullseye to check. Suddenly, Christopher leans over and smacks my water gun, knocking the steady stream off the target.

"Hey! No fair!" I attempt to steady the gun with one hand while swatting him away with the other.

"What's the matter, Michelle? Looks like you're having trouble aiming."

I laugh as I continue to fight him off. "You're cheating!"

Aiden's balloon pops and the buzzer goes off, and he slaps palms with Christopher.

I shake my head, smiling. "Fine. You can have this one, birthday boy."

"It's your birthday?" the operator of the game asks.

"Yyyes."

"Pick any prize you want."

Aiden's eyes light up. "I wwwant that one."

The man uses a long stick with a hook at the end of it to reach a set of white stuffed bears. They're holding onto a heart that's cut in a jagged line down the middle. One side of the heart reads *Best*, and the other side reads *Friends*. Aiden pulls them apart and hands one to me.

"I'm rrreally glad yyyou came tonight."

Hot tears blur my vision.

Seriously? Again with the crying?

"Thank you."

Aiden hands his half of the bear to Christopher. "Can yyyou hold this for mmme?"

Christopher's eyes look as glossy as mine. "Sure, bud. You ready for some ice cream?"

Two bites into his cup of vanilla and chocolate swirl, Aiden decides he wants to play a race car simulation game. Christopher and I sit side by side on a bench several feet away so we can keep an eye on him.

The waves crash on the beach behind us in the distance. Off-season down the shore is like seeing the real Oz, the average man behind the magic. No dazzling lights. No blaring music. No bustling crowd. Just the simplicity of the sand and the waves mixed with the crisp saltwater air.

"You know I moved Aiden here because of you," Christopher says, breaking the silence.

"What do you mean?"

"You once told me how your mom used to take you to the beach during the winter. You wouldn't have to wait on any lines to play the boardwalk games that were still open, and you'd eat cotton candy until your stomach hurt. And after——"

"She'd wrap me in a blanket while we sat on the sand and watched the waves crash." I shake my head, smiling. "I can't believe you remember all that."

"It sounded so peaceful. So simple. When I moved back home to take care of Aiden, I wanted to take him as far away as I could from all the crap he'd been through. Away from my father. Away from my sister ever finding us again." He shrugs. "This was the only place I pictured us."

I glance at Aiden. "He's such a sweet boy."

"I just want to do right by him."

"It looks like you're doing more than that."

Christopher looks down, eyebrows pinched together, deep in thought. If I could hear his thoughts, I'd bet he's thinking about how much more he wishes he could do for Aiden.

He has no clue how much he's already done.

I reach out and smooth the worry lines on his forehead with my thumb. I've done it so many times in the past, it's an involuntary gesture. But I realize my mistake as soon as it happens.

Christopher's body stills, his eyes flicking to meet mine in surprise. "You remember when you used to do that?"

I quickly drop my hand into my lap. "I've tried to forget."

"I haven't."

My heartrate speeds up as dozens of butterflies stir to life in my chest. The intensity in his gaze, the fullness of his lips, it's all right here in front of me. After all these years, I'd never expected to see him again. A part of me still can't believe he's really here.

I swallow past the lump that's lodged in my throat. "When you left, it was the only way I could move on. I had to push the memories away."

"That's funny because the memories were the only things that kept me going."

Now's your chance. Ask him.

I inhale a brave breath. "Chris, what happened?"

He sets his cup of melting ice cream on the bench and turns to face me, his warm brown eyes boring into mine, into my soul, like they always have. "When my father called me that night, he was completely loaded. I thought it was just another one of his belligerent calls. He was going on and on about my sister, and I assumed she'd gone home to hit him up for money. That's what she always did, disappear for a few months and then come back when she ran out of drug money.

"But then he said something about Aiden. As I tried to make sense of his slurred speech, I realized that my sister left Aiden on my father's porch with nothing but a backpack and a note. The kid was only eight-years old, and she left him with our alcoholic father."

He shakes his head, and his gaze drops from mine. "I knew I couldn't leave him there. I couldn't leave the kid to grow up in that kind of environment. But what was I going to do? I couldn't keep him with me in the dorms. I had to go."

"I understand all that. I really do. But why ..." My hands shake, almost too nervous to ask. "Why didn't you tell me you were leaving?"

"I couldn't drag you into my mess."

"I could've helped you."

"That's exactly why I didn't want to tell you. I had to drop out of college, Michelle. You would've wanted to come with me. You would've wanted to do it together."

"Because that's what you do when you love someone!"

Several people walking past us turn their heads in the direction of my outburst.

Christopher's expression is pained. "I didn't want that life for you. I didn't know where I would go, or what I'd end up doing. You deserve the world. I couldn't give that to you." His Adam's apple bobs up and down, and his voice is raspy when he speaks. "You deserve the kind of life a rich lawyer can give you."

A laugh rips from my throat at the same time my tears spring free. I must look maniacal, but I'm too angry to care. "Yeah, some life that is."

"What does that mean?"

"Nothing. It's not important." I wipe my cheeks with the backs of my hands. "You don't know what it was like waking up without you, not knowing where you were or what happened to you. Five years, Christopher. Five years of radio silence. Now here you are," I wave my hand around in front of me, "and you expect everything to pick up where we left off."

"I don't." He reaches out and cradles my face, his eyes filled with pain and regret. "Michelle, leaving you five years ago was the hardest thing I've ever had to do, and it hurt like hell. It still hurts. But I thought I was doing the right thing. I thought it'd be easier if I disappeared and you just forgot about me."

My bottom lip trembles. "How could you think I'd forget about you so easily?"

He leans forward and rests his forehead against mine. "I know I don't deserve your forgiveness, but I hope in time you can find it in your heart to forgive me."

"That's a lot to ask."

"I'm sorry, Bambi. I'm so sorry."

I pull back from him. "I hate it when you call me that."

"Because it reminds you of your mom, or because it reminds you of all that we had?"

"Both. It's too much. It's all too much right now."

He nods. "What you're doing for Aiden tonight is more than I deserve. I just need you to know that my leaving had nothing to do with you, and I never stopped—"

"Is everrrything okay?"

I look up into Aiden's concerned eyes. "Hey, all done with the car game?"

"Yyyeah. Arrre you two fighting?"

"No," Christopher says, standing. "We were just talking. We had a lot to catch up on. What do you want to play next?"

"I'm tirrred. Can we go hommme?"

"Are you sure?" I stand, clutching my stuffed bear. "We can play another round of air hockey if you want."

Aiden shakes his head, a sullen expression on his face. "I just wwwant to go home."

Christopher squeezes his shoulder. "Okay, bud. Let's go."

CHRISTOPHER

I watch Michelle's taillights until they disappear out of my apartment complex. Sighing heavily, I lock the door and shut off the lights in the living room.

My phone buzzes in my pocket, and my heart pounds faster, hoping it's Michelle.

Thomas Rodgers: Hope Aiden feels better soon. Let us know when you'd like to reschedule his birthday trip to the arcade. Jordan's looking forward to it.

What?

Before I respond, I walk into Aiden's bedroom, holding my phone up. "Do you know why Mr. Rodgers is texting me saying he wants you to feel better?"

Aiden's eyes go wide. "Uh ... I mmmight know sommmething about that."

I pop a brow and his shoulders slump. "I lied and told Jorrrdan that I wwwasn't feeling wwwell."

"Why on earth would you do that? You were so excited to go to the arcade with him."

"I knnnew if Jordan couldn't come, yyyou'd call Mmmichelle, and she wwwould feel bad and she'd come wwwwith us."

I drop onto the edge of his mattress, dumbfounded. "Aiden ... I don't even know what to say to that."

"I wwwas just trrrying to help yyyou."

I scrub a hand over my face. "I appreciate your concern, bud, but my problems aren't for you to worry about. You should be worrying about kid stuff. You should've been playing with Jordan tonight."

"And yyyou should've stayed at college. But yyyou left for mmme."

My gut wrenches. *That's* what this is about.

"Of course I left for you. You're my nephew. You're my responsibility."

He shakes his head. "I wwwas mmmom's responsibility. But I wwwas yyyour choice."

I hold his precious little face in my hands. "You're right. I chose you. And I'll always choose you. You don't owe me, and you don't have to worry about me and Michelle."

"I just thought it wwwould help if yyyou spent sommme time with her. I didn't wwwant you to fight." He looks down at his Captain America comforter. "I wwwanted to help yyyou like yyyou helped mmme."

God, this kid is killing me. "Aiden, it's not tit-for-tat. Family helps each other out. I don't want you to lie to me again. Understand?"

He nods, letting what I said sink in.

"That being said, that *was* a real smooth move winning that stuffed bear for Michelle."

A slow grin pulls his lips to the right. "It wwwas, rrright?"

"You're going to make some girl very happy one day."

"Yyyou think so?"

"I know so. If you were Michelle's age, I think you'd give me a run for my money. She adores you."

Aiden laughs. "She adores yyyou too."

I shake my head. "She used to."

"She still does. She wwwouldn't have cried tonight if she didn't like yyyou."

"Are you sure you're only thirteen and not thirty?" I slap my palm to my forehead. "Oh! That reminds me!"

I bolt out of his room and return a few seconds later. "Here's your birthday present."

Aiden can't hide his excitement as he tears into the Marvel wrapping paper. Popping the top of the box open, his eyebrows pull together as he gazes inside. "This wwwatch looks expensive."

"It's priceless, actually." I lift the watch out of the box and slip it onto his bony wrist. I'll have to take a few more links out than I thought. "My mom gave me this watch on my thirteenth birthday. It was my grandfather's. Now I'm passing it down to you."

Aiden's eyes widen as he looks up at me. "Yyyou should keep it. Yyyou might have your own son sommmeday. You should give it to himmm."

I place my hand on his shoulder, making sure he looks me in my eyes when I say this: "Aiden, I know I'm not your biological father, but as far as I'm concerned, you are just like a son to me. And I want you to have this watch."

A tear rolls down his cheek, and he dips his head so that I don't see.

I pretend I don't notice a thing. It's Bro Code.

"Can wwwe watch *Buffy*?" he asks.

We've been watching the entire series, from start to finish.

I clap him on the back and stand. "I thought you'd never ask."

10

MICHELLE

"What's that?"

I glance over at the bear sitting on my nightstand and smile. "Aiden won it for me last night on the boardwalk."

Richard nods. "Aiden, the handicapped boy?"

"No. Aiden. Just Aiden."

"He's the one with the handicap, isn't he?"

"Yes, but you don't have to call him that. His name is Aiden."

Richard bends down and places a chaste kiss on my forehead. "Okay, babe." Then he steps into the bathroom and nods toward the shower. "Want to join me?"

I turn my back to him and continue putting the laundry away. "No."

Instead of walking up behind me and kissing my neck, apologizing, or coaxing me into the shower with him, he shuts the bathroom door and goes about his business.

Why does he have to be so cold?

He's always been this way. That's what you wanted.

He's been worse lately.

No. You're going soft, crying all the time and shit.

Well, I'm done with that. No more crying.

Oh, yeah? Look at that bear again. Bet you five bucks you tear up.

Buzzing across the room snaps me out of my insanity. I snatch my cell phone off my nightstand without making eye-contact with the stuffed bear who's smiling up at me.

"Hey, Raegan?"

"Hey! What are you up to?"

"Doing laundry. Ugh."

"Well, I know it's Sunday night, and we're supposed to be doing lesson plans, but I need to get out. Would you want to grab a drink?"

"Absolutely," I say too quickly.

She chuckles. "Are you sure? You're not busy with your man or anything?"

Richard is home before dinnertime for the first night all week. I should want to stay home and spend time with him. I should want to talk over dinner, cuddle on the couch while we watch a movie.

Then I remember that he'll be busy watching Sunday night football, and I'll be non-existent.

Fuck it. "No, he's got football to keep him busy."

"I certainly don't miss those days. Text me your address."

I send Rae my address, jump off the bed, and stick my head into the steamy bathroom. "I'm meeting a friend for drinks. I'll be back in a couple hours."

* * *

"THIS IS EXACTLY WHAT I NEEDED."

Raegan raises her margarita in the air. "To Mexican food and good friends."

I clink my glass against hers and take a long gulp of my mango margarita. "Have you been to this place before?"

"Only once, when I was with my ex-husband."

"How long were you two married?"

"Seven years."

"Wow. What happened, if you don't mind my asking?"

She shakes her head, her blond waves falling over her shoulders.

"I don't mind at all. I guess I got married too young. The person I was when we first met wasn't the same person I ended up growing into."

"Why do you think you changed?"

She spins the stem of her glass, deep in thought. "I think we all change. It's inevitable not to. There are so many layers to us, so many life experiences to learn from. You learn as you go, and sometimes you find that what you once wanted isn't what you want anymore. And that's okay."

"Is it?"

Her green eyes narrow as she tilts her head to the side. "Are you asking me, or yourself?"

I shrug. "Both, I guess."

"You have to give yourself permission to change. Give yourself permission to grow into who you're meant to be. If you're with the right person, he'll grow with you."

"And if you're not?"

"Then he'll stifle you. Don't ever let anyone stifle you, including yourself." She takes a sip of her drink. "We can be our own worst enemies."

"Don't I know it," I say with a humorless laugh. "This might sound crazy but I have this voice inside me that I swear is out to get me. It's like she argues about every decision I make. She drives me nuts."

"That's your inner bitch," Raegan says. "You need her. Listen to her. She's there for a reason. Lord knows I should've listened to mine sooner than I did."

My eyebrows shoot up. "You hear voices too?"

"I mean, I'm not seeing dead people or anything. But the voice that tells you what to do? That's your gut. Your woman's intuition. She needs to be set free. You'll go nuts if you keep her locked up for too long, like those women who snap and kill people for no reason." She raises her glass to her lips. "There's always a reason. They didn't listen to their inner bitches."

I stare down into my drink for a while.

"What's your inner bitch telling you to do?"

I drag my eyes up to hers, too afraid to say it out loud. "I don't know. I think I'm just really stressed out lately."

Liar.

"That's understandable. You're a first-year teacher." She gestures to my engagement ring. "And you're planning a wedding. That's enough stress to choke a horse."

"I actually haven't started planning it yet."

"What are you waiting for?"

I shrug, averting my gaze again. "It feels weird doing it without my mom."

Raegan's hand covers mine. "Did she pass?"

I nod. "She died so long ago, you'd think this wouldn't be an issue. But I'd always imagined my mom being there on my wedding day, and now it's happening without her."

"I'm so sorry. For what it's worth, I'm here. I can help you. I planned a wedding. Granted, the marriage didn't last, but the wedding was bomb as fuck!"

I laugh, and it feels good.

We order a few appetizers and another round of drinks, talking and laughing about work.

"What happened after the dodgeball game? I would've been mortified if I knocked Principal Waters out like that."

Raegan's cheeks turn a rosy shade of red. "He knew it was an accident."

"I was right at the costume store, right? Something's going on between you two."

She hesitates before answering, but her eyes tell me all I need to know.

I nod in understanding. "It's okay. I won't tell a soul."

"It's complicated. We met over the summer. I was out with my friends celebrating my divorce. I'd had way too much to drink, and he was there in that damn suit."

Oh, shit. Raegan boned the boss.

The man does look incredible in a suit.

She grimaces. "I had no idea he would be our new principal. I had no idea ..." she trails off. "It's awkward, to say the least."

"I can imagine."

She gives me a knowing smirk. "Kind of like it is for you and Chris?"

Mango and tequila go down the wrong pipe, and I sputter and choke for the next minute.

"I'll take that as a yes," she says.

"It's complicated," I croak out.

Raegan giggles. "I told you my secret. It's your turn."

I slump forward, resting my chin in my hand. "We dated in college."

Her eyebrows shoot up. "Okay, I know there's more to that story."

"Oh, there is. But I'm going to need another drink if I'm going to tell it."

She grabs the waiter's attention as he passes by. "Excuse me. We'll take another round. And keep 'em coming."

Another two margaritas go down like water, and now I can't feel my legs.

"I knew it," Raegan says after I finish telling her about Christopher. She twists her hair into a top knot and shakes her head. "I knew there was something between you two. I saw it in the way he looked at you at the Halloween store."

I lean forward, my glossy eyes wide. "How did he look at me?"

She clutches her chest and squeezes her eyes shut. I can't tell if she's swaying or if I am. "He looks at you like you're the only one in the room. Like he'd give anything to wrap his arms around you and keep you there forever."

I sigh. "I used to love it when he looked at me like that. Now, it just makes me angry."

"How does Richard look at you?"

"From behind a computer screen," I blurt out.

"Ouch."

"Yeah. He works a lot."

"That doesn't bother you?"

"It never used to. But ..."

"But now Christopher's back in the picture."

I cover my face with my hands. "He broke my heart. I shouldn't give two shits about him. We dated five years ago. That was like another lifetime ago."

"Love doesn't waver with time."

"I've moved on."

"Have you though?"

I close one eye and point my index finger at her. "You sound like my inner bitch."

"Look, I'm not trying to sway you one way or the other. But it's my job as your new, self-proclaimed best friend to tell you the truth."

I sit back in my chair and brace myself. "All right. Let me have it."

"Don't make the same mistakes I made. You can't get married to someone if your heart belongs to someone else. I don't know Richard, and I'm not in your relationship. But if your gut is telling you that something's missing with him, then maybe you should listen. Maybe you and Christopher ending up in the same place isn't just a coincidence."

I'm quiet as the waiter deposits our check on the table.

Raegan insists on paying, and we agree that I'll pay the next time. It makes me happy to know that we'll be going out again. I really enjoyed her company.

We stumble into the parking lot to wait for our Uber driver.

"You know what?" Raegan asks.

"What?"

"This might be overstepping, but I've just gotta say this: I'm Team Christopher. Richard Smichard."

I snort. "Smichard."

"Mr. and Mrs. Smichard."

I double over with laughter, grasping onto her forearm. "Don't make me laugh. I'm going to pee myself."

We cackle like the drunk morons we are until a black SUV pulls up to the curb. "Are you Raegan?"

Raegan salutes him "Yes, sir."

"Why did you just salute him?" I whisper.

"I don't know," she whispers back.

We climb into the back seat and Raegan rests her head on my shoulder the entire way. Before we roll up to Richard's apartment, she says, "In all seriousness, Chris is a great guy."

Sighing, I close my eyes. "I know, Rae. I know."

"He deserves the world after what he's done for Aiden. And they're a package deal. So if you hurt Chris, you're hurting Aiden too. Just try to keep that in mind, whatever you do."

11

CHRISTOPHER

"What the hell does this even mean?" Aiden drops his forehead onto the table. "I don't knnnow."

What kind of math is this? This looks nothing like anything I've ever learned. "Okay, let me read it again: Jimmy needs forty-two watermelons for a party." I pause, looking at Aiden. "Who needs that many watermelons?"

"Apparently Jimmmmy."

"Well, Jimmy's an idiot."

"Can I wrrrite that on the test?"

"Please don't." I heave a frustrated sigh, pulling at the ends of my hair. "You're going to need a tutor. I can call Rae and ask her if she's available."

Aiden reaches into his pants pocket and pulls out his phone. I watch as his thumbs tap dance across the screen.

"Put the phone away until you finish your homework."

"I wwwas just texting Mmmichelle to see if she wwwwants to be mmmy tutor."

My jaw drops open. "You what? How do you have her number?"

"Yyyou really nnneed a better password on yyyour phone."

This kid is going to be the death of me.

I'm about to lecture him about privacy when his phone vibrates on the table. I lean over his shoulder. "What did she say?"

He laughs. "Thought yyyou didn't wwwant her to tutor mmme."

I playfully push his head. "Just read the text."

Aiden grins. "She asked wwwhy mmmy geek of an uncle can't tutor mmme."

Of all the nerve.

With a huff, I pull out my phone and type out a text to Michelle:

Me: This Common Core math is no joke

Michelle: You're a Brainiac. And a teacher. I'm sure you can figure it out.

Me: I'm a gym teacher, remember? We play with balls all day

Me: OK I realize that sounds wrong

Me: But seriously ... who needs to buy 42 watermelons? What kind of party is this? And how is he transporting all these watermelons once he buys them? I have questions, damnit!

Michelle: I can't even pretend to know what you're rambling about.

Me: Full disclosure, I can't pay you much if you agree to tutor. I understand if you don't want to do it

Michelle: I'm not taking your money. It's for Aiden. Don't worry about it.

Michelle: When do I start?

Me: When are you available?

Michelle: I can be there in 20min.

Aiden claps me on the shoulder. "Yyyou're wwwelcome."

I shake my head. "You're turning into quite the wingman."

"You should mmmake that shrimmmp dish for dinner. The one wwwith the pasta."

"Oh, now she's staying for dinner?"

He shrugs. "If yyyou're nnnot going to pay her, the least yyyou can do is cook her dinner."

The kid has a point. "Keep working on your homework until she gets here."

I pull the shrimp out of the freezer and set the rest of the ingredients on the counter, all the while trying to ignore the swarm of killer bees buzzing around in my stomach.

She's engaged to someone else.

She's engaged to someone else.

She's engaged to someone else.

Maybe if I say it enough times, it'll sink in.

My phone vibrates in my pocket, and when I check who's calling, the bees stop buzzing.

I make a mad dash for my bedroom, and click the lock after I close the door.

"Hey, Phil. How's it going?"

Phil's gruff voice barks through the phone. "Hiya, kid. I got a hit on a woman down in Tennessee this morning. I'm flying down to check it out."

"What makes you think it's her?"

"Fits the description. 'Bout an hour north of your old man's place."

I nod, even though he can't see me. "I'd hate for you to go on another wild goose chase."

"Ah, it's in the job description. I'll keep you posted."

The call ends before I can say anything more.

I sink down onto the corner of my mattress, gripping onto the comforter for support.

What if it's her?

What if she wants him back?

What if he doesn't want to live with me anymore?

I jump at the knock on the door. "She's here," Aiden calls.

"Okay. Be out in a sec." I inhale through my nose and exhale through my mouth, trying to gather my thoughts.

When I enter the living room, I plaster a smile on my face. "Hey, Michelle. Thanks again for coming."

She eyes me suspiciously from her seat next to Aiden, those doe eyes seeing right through me. "No problem."

"This is the mmmath problem wwwe couldn't figure out," Aiden says.

"All right. Let's see what Jimmy wants to do with all these watermelons."

I leave them to it, and head into the kitchen to start dinner. I toss the garlic into the pan, hands shaking, and steal another peek at Aiden.

He laughs at something she said, and then she high-fives him. His face lights up like a Christmas tree whenever he's with her. Being with her is the happiest I've seen him. Maybe it's crazy, but having Michelle here with us feels right. Like this is the way things should be. Like we're meant to be a family.

Then realization slams into me like a freight train.

Aiden's been trying so hard to get me back with Michelle, but what if it doesn't work out? What will happen to that goofy smile on his face?

He's getting attached, and I let it happen.

Michelle's with someone else. She'll be making her own family one day.

With Dick.

Whenever I picture them together, my heart feels like it's being torn from my chest.

I can't imagine what it'll be like when it actually happens.

What Aiden will feel.

I only hope we can withstand it.

MICHELLE

Christopher looks so natural in this role as caretaker.

I give him a lot of credit. Not many young men in their twenties could do this. I can't picture my brother Michael taking care of me in addition to himself.

The guy can barely make himself a bowl of cereal.

"Need any help?" I ask, standing beside Christopher at the small counter.

"Nope. Dinner should be ready in a few."

"Aiden's taking a practice quiz on what I just taught him." I turn my back to the counter and hoist myself up. "Mind if I watch you?"

"Not at all. I can take my shirt off if you'd like." He grins and wiggles his eyebrows.

"God, no. Your luck, you'll spill hot oil on yourself and I'll have to rush you to the hospital with third degree burns."

He chuckles. "Good point."

Warmth pools in my chest when I picture him cooking with nothing but his low-slung jeans on. Bare chest, smooth skin, muscles rippling in front of the stove.

How does someone wearing a bright yellow oven mitt look so sexy?

"You okay?" he asks. "You look a little flush."

I swallow hard and avert my gaze to Aiden. "Yes, I'm fine."

"I appreciate your help. I'm sure you have better things to do than hang around here with us."

"I don't mind," I say, and it's the truth. "I'm happy to help."

"Aiden loves being around you." Christopher sets the wooden spoon down on the counter and turns to face me. "Not gonna lie, I do too."

This time, I can't look away from him, those warm, cavernous eyes of his pinning me down.

It's as if we're two sparks on opposite sides of a rope, headed straight for a giant bomb in the middle. I don't know how much time it'll take until we combust, or what'll happen when we do. But it feels like it's inevitable.

Heat rolls off Christopher as his gaze drops to my mouth. The passion, the want, the tortured restraint in his eyes—it's all sizzling in the air between us. He reaches out and his fingers graze my cheek, the touch so light it causes me to lean into him just to feel more of it. My chest rises and falls, but I'm barely able to breathe. It feels like forever since I've felt like this, since my body reacted to someone this way.

Actually, he *was* the last person who made me feel this way.

"Wwwhat's that smmmell?" Aiden asks.

"Shit!" Christopher rushes to the sink with flames shooting up from his oven mitt. He yanks the lever on the faucet and tosses the mitt into the sink.

I jump down from the counter. "Are you okay? Did you get burned?"

He runs the water over his hand. "No. I don't think so."

"Let me see." I turn his hand over, inspecting it.

"There goes another mmmitt," Aiden calls.

"Another?" I raise an eyebrow at Christopher. "You mean this isn't the first time you've set yourself on fire?"

He pops a careless shoulder. "Guess it's a good thing you didn't let me take my shirt off after all."

I huff out a laugh, shaking my head. "Come on, Aiden. Let's set the table before your uncle kills us all."

* * *

"Thank you for dinner."

"If you won't let me pay you, at least I can feed you."

I shake my head. "I couldn't take your money, Christopher."

Aiden insisted on cleaning up after we finished eating, and it's not lost on me that he's currently nowhere to be found. The kid is perceptive.

"I truly appreciate your help," Christopher says. "You don't know how many times a day I ask myself if I'm doing the right thing by him."

"How could you even question that? You're so good with him."

Christopher blows a stream of air through his nostrils. "Look around. This kid deserves better. He deserves more. I often wonder if he'd have been better off in foster care."

"Don't do that. Don't act like you're not the best thing to happen to him. God only knows where he would've ended up with the way the system is." I shudder at the thought. "You're who he needs to be with. Even if you did set yourself on fire."

The corner of his mouth ticks. "Yeah, well, I was distracted. You can't blame me."

Warmth envelops my body. I play with a thread on my jeans just to keep myself from getting sucked into his gaze again.

"Can I tell you something?" he asks.

Anything. "Sure."

He glances to the hallway as he lowers his voice. "A few years ago, I hired a private investigator to find my sister."

My jaw pops open. "Really? Why?"

"I was hoping one day she'd get her shit together, get clean. When I left Tennessee, I didn't tell my dad where I was taking Aiden. If my sister ever came back to look for him, she wouldn't be able to find us. I wasn't sure if I'd made the right decision. So I hired someone to keep tabs on her. Only, we haven't been able to find her."

His eyes drop to his hands in his lap. "Before you came over today, the PI called. He said he found someone in Tennessee who fits her description."

My heartrate speeds up. "What happens if it's her?"

"I don't know. I guess it depends what shape she's in."

"If she's clean."

He nods. "What if she's looking for him? What if she's clean and she wants her son back?"

"Then she shouldn't have left him," I snap.

Christopher offers me a small smile. "She's his mother."

"It's not the same. She's not like our mothers." I cross my arms over my chest. "What does Aiden think of this?"

His eyes look straight into mine. "He doesn't know."

"Well, I think he should have a say in whether his crackhead mother comes back into his life."

Christopher's large hand covers my balled-up fist, and his dimpled grin spreads wide. "It seems like he's not the only one I have to worry about getting too attached here."

He's right. You're getting attached.

What am I doing here? I finished tutoring Aiden over an hour ago. I should've left after dinner.

You don't want to.

"I should go home," I say, my voice just above a whisper.

"It feels like you are home." His hand cups my face, his thumb gently stroking my cheekbone. "Doesn't it?"

I squeeze my eyes shut, so as not to look into those dangerous hazel eyes of his. "Chris, please. Don't."

"Don't what?"

"Don't make this harder than it already is."

"Nothing's harder than seeing you with someone else."

My eyes pop open, searing holes through his. "You made this happen."

"Then let me make it right." He takes both of my hands in his, gripping onto them. "Please, Michelle. Let me fix this. I'll do anything. Just tell me it's not too late."

A tear rolls down my cheek, and I make no effort to swipe it away. I lift my chin and rise from the chair, sliding my hands out of his grasp. "It's too late, Christopher."

Before he can stop me, I'm out the door and in my car, sobbing the entire way home.

CHRISTOPHER

I whip my pillow at the beeping alarm clock.

Satanic little invention.

"Yyyou already hit snooze three timmmes."

I jolt at the sound of Aiden's voice. "Go back to bed. Let's take a sick day."

"Can't. I have a mmmath test."

I dig the heels of my hands into my eyes and sigh. "Why do you have to be such a good kid?"

He grins. "Commme on. Wwwe're gonna be late."

Late.

That's an understatement.

It's too late, Christopher.

Michelle's words rang in my ears all night.

I laid it all on the line for her. Practically begged for another chance. She was right there, close enough for me to touch, tears in her eyes like she felt my pain.

But it's too late.

I'm too late.

She's marrying someone else.

Aiden eyes me as I throw the covers off my body and stand. "Yyyou okay, Uncle Chris?"

I shake my head. "No, bud. I'm not. But I will be."

I skip a shower, opting to wallow in my stench of body odor and self-pity for the day.

I don't stop at Dunkin Donuts on the way to work. I don't visit Michelle's classroom. I go about my day like I always used to, before she walked through those doors.

Better get used to it.

* * *

"Does everybody understand the rules?"

"Yes, Mr. Hastings."

I blow into my whistle and the gymnasium fills with screams. It's the one place kids are allowed to yell inside the school, and they don't take it for granted. I don't mind. They learn the most when they're having fun. And that's the number one rule in my gym.

Their screams are so loud, I don't hear the clack of Michelle's shoes on the old wooden floor. I smell her before I see her, her sweet, flowery scent impossible to forget. Not even after all these years.

Time has done nothing to dull the memory of *her*.

I'm not sure it ever could.

My heart leaps out of my chest at the sight of her standing beside me. Her long dark hair cascades down past her shoulders, such a contrast to her light skin. She's in an emerald-green silky blouse and black dress pants, black glasses sitting on the bridge of her turned-up nose.

God, she's beautiful.

It's too late, Christopher.

"Hey." She offers me a small smile.

"Hey."

She averts her eyes to the children playing volleyball. "They look like they're having fun."

111

"They practice with beach balls until they learn how to play the game. Then we switch to volleyballs."

She nods, and awkward silence ensues. Her eyes return to mine, and I can see the worry swirling inside her chestnut-colored irises.

"So, what's up?" I ask.

"I, uh, wanted to see what Aiden was doing this weekend."

"You don't have to tutor on the weekend. You need a break from kids and school stuff."

She pushes her glasses up her nose. "I actually wanted to invite him to come paintballing with me and my brothers."

My eyebrows shoot up. "Paintballing?"

"I know it doesn't seem like the best idea for someone like him, but I also know how much Aiden wants to do the things that all the other kids do." She shrugs. "You can come too if you want."

"I think he'd love that. I'm just not so sure about putting him in harm's way like that. He's more fragile than the average kid, and getting shot with a paintball hurts."

"I get it," she says. "But my brothers would take it easy on him. He could guard the flag, hide in the tree house or something. This way, he wouldn't have to worry about maneuvering with the gun and his crutches."

A small smile pulls at my lips. "You've put a lot of thought into this."

A pink blush tinges her cheeks. "I think he could use some fun in his life."

I nod, letting the idea settle into my mind. "I guess it would be—"

A beach ball slams into the side of my face, cutting off the rest of my sentence.

Michelle jumps back, covering her mouth with her hand, while the class freezes on the court.

"Sorry, Mr. Hastings!" McKenzie, one of the third graders, runs over to retrieve the ball. "Are you okay?"

I chuckle as I hand the ball to her. "I'm fine, Rebecca. Thank you for asking. Try to keep the ball on the court."

"Yes, sir. Sorry, sir."

I blow the whistle when she takes her spot to serve the ball, and the game continues.

I offer Michelle a sheepish smile. "Bet you enjoyed that."

She shakes her head, amusement dancing in her eyes. "You are so accident prone."

"You used to love that about me."

"I also used to love bangs, but I learned from that mistake."

I clutch my chest and stagger backward. "Ouch."

She rolls her eyes, but she's smiling. "So, what do you say?"

I shove my hands into my pockets and heave a sigh. "I guess we're going paintballing."

* * *

"GOOD WORK TODAY, AIDEN."

Aiden grins. "Thanks, Dr. Mmmartin."

"Can you please step out into the waiting room so I can talk to your uncle?"

Aiden huffs a sigh. He hates when doctors make him leave the room just to talk about him.

He closes the door behind him, and I turn my attention to Dr. Martin. "Everything okay, Doc'?"

He rolls his chair around the examination table. "Yes, yes. Everything's fine. I wanted to talk to you about *you*, actually."

"Me?"

"How are you doing, Christopher?"

"Uh, I'm fine. Why do you ask?"

"Aiden isn't progressing in his therapy as much as I'd like him to. Usually, when I see this, it's because the child's parent is holding him or her back from doing more. It's common to be overly careful and feel worried about Aiden's well-being. But he's capable of a lot more than you realize. I'd like to push him a little further."

My eyebrows dip down as I ingest his words. "What do you suggest? He can't exactly try out for the football team."

"No, of course not. But activities like swimming, climbing on a jungle gym, or even a slow jog on a treadmill can help. I know he's at the age where kids stay inside playing video games all day, but it's important to keep Aiden moving."

I nod. "I can do that."

He stands, extending his arm for a handshake. "You're doing a great job with him, Chris. You should be proud."

Yeah. Proud.

I'm the reason Aiden isn't progressing.

I'm holding him back.

Every day, I wonder if I'm doing right by Aiden. I don't know the first thing about raising a child, being a parent. I had a great mother figure for a chunk of my childhood, but she's not here now. I can't ask her questions, can't bounce things off of her. And my father was good for nothing. Still is.

I'm doing this all on my own.

And it feels like I'm in way over my head.

13

MICHELLE

"How are you feeling?"

I fumble with the strap on my chest guard, my fingers shaking. "I'd feel better if I could get this thing tighter."

Michael rests his hands over mine. "Relax, Michelle." He tugs the strap out of my grasp and adjusts it until it's snug around my waist. "Better?"

I nod, averting my gaze from his knowing eyes. "Yup. All better."

"This is going to be epic!" Ryan shouts, aiming his paintball gun at the trees.

"Yeah, an epic fail," Caleb retorts. "You're going down, brother!"

The two drop their guns onto the dead leaves and lunge at each other. Ryan puts Caleb in a headlock while Caleb punches him in the ribs.

Michael shakes his head. "You sure you want Christopher to witness your crazy family?"

"This isn't about Christopher. It's about Aiden."

Michael holds his hands up on either side of his head. "Whatever you say, sis'."

I grunt, the heat from my breath puffing out into the November air. My body is shivering, but it's not from the cold. Was this a good idea, introducing Christopher to my family? It sounded fine at the time when I thought of it. I couldn't invite Aiden without asking Chris to come along too. But this is personal. This is my family.

And I'm supposed to be separating myself from Christopher, not pulling him further into my life.

Christopher and Aiden appear on the dirt path through the trees, and my stomach knots itself even tighter.

Michael kicks Ryan in his ass. "Cut it out," he hisses. "They're here."

Ry and Caleb have no idea who Christopher is, or what he means to me. All they know is how important this outing is for Aiden.

Decked out in army fatigues, Aiden's face is beaming as he makes his way toward us. "Hey, Mmmichelle."

My smile matches his as the stress rolls off my shoulders. *This* is why I'm doing this. His smile is worth everything.

"Hey, Cap'." I sling my arm over his shoulders. "Guys, this is Aiden. Aiden, these are my brothers."

He shifts his weight, uncuffing his right arm from the crutch, and extends his hand to Michael. "It's nnnice to mmmeet you."

Michael's smile is huge as he clasps Aiden's hand. Even Ryan and Caleb manage to pull themselves together and appear eerily respectful as they each shake Aiden's hand next.

Michael swings his hand to Christopher. "You must be Chris. Glad you could make it today."

I don't miss his overly-firm grip around Christopher's hand. I bite my bottom lip to stifle a laugh. Such a good big brother.

"Thanks for inviting us," Christopher says. "We've never been paintballing before."

I tap his helmet with my knuckles. "Good thing you've got protective gear."

He smirks. "I'll still manage to get hurt somehow."

I shake my head and let the smile bloom on my face. "I don't doubt that."

"Here are your walkie-talkies." Caleb's friend, George, passes a duffle bag around the group. "Me, Ry, Will, and Caleb will be on Channel 1. You four can switch yours onto Channel 2."

Caleb hands a yellow flag to Aiden. "Here's your team flag. I hear you'll be the one guarding it."

Aiden lifts his chin, puffing out his chest. "You heard right."

"All right. First team to capture the other team's flag is the winner."

We pull our visors down over our faces and switch on our walkies.

"May the best team win!" Ryan walks backwards with both middle fingers in the air and a devilish grin.

He and Caleb dart into the woods with their friends close behind. Michael, Christopher, Aiden, and I head in the opposite direction to hide our flag.

"I've been here before," Michael says. "There's a tree house up ahead. Aiden, think you can climb up there and guard the flag?"

His eyes light up. "Yes!"

Christopher shoots me a worried glance. I squeeze his arm and lean in to whisper, "He'll be okay."

"I'll be like a sniper!" Aiden says.

Michael grins. "Perfect. Michelle, you can guard the area below him. Chris, you'll come with me to capture the blue team's flag."

"Do you know how to use the gun?" I ask Christopher.

"Sure. How hard can it be? Just point and—" Before he can say *shoot*, yellow paint splats onto his shoe.

"Ow! God, that hurts!" His face reddens as he continues to mumble a string of expletives.

I cringe, turning to Michael. "You might have to protect him from himself as opposed to the other team."

"Yyyou sure yyyou don't wwwant Uncle Chris in the tree house innnstead?" Aiden asks.

Michael chuckles, patting Christopher on the back. "Don't worry, man. I've got your back. Let's go."

Christopher limps after him as they disappear into the compound, leaving me and Aiden to hide the flag.

"Well, Cap', looks like it's just me and you."

Aiden hasn't stopped smiling. "Commme on, Bucky. Wwwe have to get to the tree house."

I'll admit, I'm a little concerned about Aiden climbing up a ladder to get into the tree house. And when I see how high up it is, my stomach twists.

"You sure you'll be able to get up there?" I ask.

Aiden nods. "Hold mmmy crutches. Yyyou can brrring them up after."

I watch helplessly as Aiden struggles to pull himself up each rung. His arms do most of the work, and his left leg drags behind him. But not once does he stop or quit. With furrowed brows and his tongue between his teeth, he's determined to get up there. I stay below him, prepared to catch him if he falls. But he doesn't. Aiden makes it all the way up the ladder and takes his gun from me before crawling inside the tree house.

That kid is my hero.

My walkie-talkie crackles just before Aiden's voice comes through. "This is Cap' to Bucky. Do yyyou copy?"

I smile and click the button on the side. "Nice work getting up that ladder, Cap'."

"Are you okay, Aiden?" Christopher's voice comes through this time.

"Yyyes, I'm finnne. Are yyyou okay?"

"He hasn't shot himself again, if that's what you're asking," Michael says.

I chuckle and press the button again. "Okay, the flag is hidden. I'm going to get into position. Over and out."

"Watch your back, Bambi. Keep my boy safe."

I run from tree to tree until I find one wide enough to hide behind. I crouch down and stare out into the woods, watching for any movement around the tree house.

There were some drawbacks to being the only girl in a house of boys growing up. There was a constant stench in the house from their smelly-ass farts. They'd always wrestle and break shit. I had no one to talk to about my period, no one to show me how to apply make-up.

But we always did fun things together. And I'd take paintballing over manicures any day.

Richard would never be caught dead paintballing.

It's true. He's too busy working to have any fun.

But Christopher is here.

Christopher would rather play a shooting video game than be out here actually getting shot at. Yet he's here. For Aiden. He's self-less and caring, and he puts family before anyone else.

He's going to make an amazing father someday.

My chest aches at the thought.

Blue paint splatters on the ground inches from my feet.

I scramble for my walkie, eyes darting around the area. "They're here! Over."

Another spray of paint shoots past me. These fuckers can see me, but I can't see them. I move around to the other side of the tree and spot Caleb and George creeping toward the tree house. I aim and fire a series of shots.

"Fuck, Caleb's hit!" George shouts into his walkie. "We need back-up!"

George disappears behind a tree, and I lose my shot. I raise the walkie to my lips. "Cap', there's one right below you, behind the shed. If you get a clear shot, take it."

"Wwwon't that give away mmmy position?" he asks.

"Not if you hit your target. I trust you. You can do this."

"Rrroger that," he says.

The end of Aiden's gun pokes through the window in the tree house. George spots him, so I have to cause a diversion. As he turns around to aim, I fire several shots. They whiz past his head and he hits the ground, crawling back behind the shed.

"I'm going to make a run for it," I say into the walkie. "As soon as he turns to me, blast him in his back."

"Donnn't get shot," Aiden says.

I run out into the clearing below the tree house, putting me right in front of the shed. "I'm coming for you, George!"

He peers around the wall of the shed, and takes a step forward to shoot me. I cringe, bracing myself for the impact of his shot, but yellow paint rains down from above.

George hits the ground, howling in pain. "Son of a bitch! I'm hit!"

"Woohoo!" I jump up and down before shouting into the walkie. "Two down, boys! Captain America saves the day!"

Aiden's worried voice booms over the speaker. "Mmmichelle, someone's commming!"

I spin around and see Ryan charging toward me. I dive behind the shed while the sound of paint balls smack against the wood.

When it goes quiet again, I hold my breath and peer around the shed. Coast is clear. Creeping forward, I edge closer to the base of the tree house. I need a clear shot in case Ryan tries to climb the ladder.

It's dead silent, which is not a good sign. My heart pounds against my chest, adrenaline coursing through my veins.

Suddenly, Ryan jumps out from behind the shed—scaring the ever-loving shit out of me—but before his finger can pull the trigger, he's shot in the back.

Christopher emerges from behind a bunker, lifting his visor and grinning wide. He raises the walkie to his lips and says, "Three down."

Dear God, that man is sexy.

I'm digging his whole camo-and-boots look. Guess that's what happens when you grow up surrounded by G.I. Joes instead of Ken dolls.

"Penny for your thoughts, Bambi," Christopher says as he approaches.

I glare at him, ignoring the heat stealing up my neck and into my cheeks. "Where's Michael?"

"He's waiting for us. We know where their flag is, but your brother's friend has good aim."

"Let's get Aiden down from the tree house. He should be the one to fire the victory shot."

Christopher's eyes travel up the length of the tree house. "He really got up there by himself?"

I smile proudly. "He did. The kid's amazing."

"Yeah, he really is."

We walk to the base of the tree and I yell up to Aiden. "Let's go win this game."

Aiden tosses down his gun, and Christopher waits for him at the bottom of the ladder.

"I'll take forrrever wwwalking there wwwith mmmy crutches," he says. "Yyyou guys can go on ahead of mmme."

"No way." Christopher turns around and kneels down. "Get on."

Aiden laughs and wraps his arms around Christopher's neck as he's hoisted up for a piggy-back ride.

"Freedom!" Christopher shouts before taking off.

I hold Aiden's crutches while the boys charge into the woods, taking my heart with them.

14

CHRISTOPHER

Aiden hasn't stopped talking about the paintball game all week. All I've ever wanted is to keep him healthy and safe. But now all I feel is tremendous guilt. I've been keeping him from doing exciting things out of fear.

My own selfish fear.

People don't realize how easy it is to assume things about disabled people, and how often we treat them differently without even realizing it.

It's accidental discrimination.

It's ignorant.

It's unacceptable.

Michelle's brothers treated Aiden like he was an average kid. They didn't look at him like a disabled boy with crutches. They didn't offer to help him carry anything.

I'll never forget the look on his face when they lifted him up and chanted his name after he took out Will and won the game.

I need to do better. I need to do more. Aiden deserves to live as normal of a life as he can.

A text from Michelle pulls me out of my thoughts as I pull up to my apartment.

. . .

Michelle: How would you feel about a change of scenery for tutoring today?

Me: Name the place and we'll be there.

Michelle: My dad's house. Aiden can play video games with Ry and Caleb afterwards, and my dad's making his famous lasagna for dinner.

Michelle: So you don't have to risk setting yourself on fire.

As much as I love the idea of spending more time with Michelle, I can't help but feel like I'm digging my own grave. Being around her, being around her family, only makes me want her more.

And I can't have her.

She's made that clear.

It's too late.

But Aiden loved hanging out with her brothers. And he loves being with Michelle. I can't let my own issues stand in the way of his fun.

So I put the car in reverse and pull away from the curb.

"Wwwhere are wwwe going?" Aiden asks.

"Michelle invited us to her dad's house for dinner. She'll tutor you and then you can play video games with the boys after."

His eyes turn into saucers. "This is gonna be awesommme!"

* * *

"This is the best lasagnnna I've everrr had," Aiden says.

Michelle's father, Dan, smiles, the swells of his round cheeks pushing his eyes almost fully closed. "Thank you. It's my wife's secret family recipe."

"Dad always makes enough for an army," Michelle says. "You'll have plenty to take for leftovers."

"Feeding you is like feeding a small army," I say.

Michelle sticks her tongue out at me from across the table.

"He's not wrong, Michy." Dan chuckles. "Out of all of us, I'd say she has the biggest appetite."

She rolls her eyes and smiles. "Sure, Dad. Take his side."

"Where's Dick tonight?" Caleb asks.

Several forks screech across the plates, and Michael kicks Caleb under the table.

"Ow! What the hell was that for?"

"Shut up and eat your lasagna, ass hat," Michael warns.

"It's fine," Michelle says, eyes dropping to her food. "Richard is working on an important case. He won't be home until late tonight."

"As usual," Ryan mutters.

"Enough," Dan says, raising his voice. "Christopher, Michelle says you're the gym teacher at her school. How long have you been working there?"

"This is my third year, sir."

"Have you always lived here in New Jersey?"

"No, sir. I moved here a few years ago from Tennessee."

Caleb takes a swig of his soda and wipes his mouth with the back of his hand, letting out a loud belch.

"Caleb, we have guests!" Michelle shakes her head, looking at me. "I'm so sorry. He's still not housebroken."

I chuckle. "It's fine. That was pretty tame compared to some of Aiden's burps."

"Let's hear it, Aiden!" Ryan says.

Aiden gulps down half his glass of soda before expelling a deep belch from his gut.

Michael claps. "That's pretty impressive, dude."

Ryan and Caleb attempt to out-do him, and for the next few minutes, a burping contest ensues. It ends when Dan surprises us all and lets out a Richter-scale-worthy belch, putting everyone at the table to shame.

Michelle's cheeks are bright red.

After dinner, Caleb and Ryan take Aiden to their shared room to play video games. Michelle and I clear off the table and Michael does the dishes while Dan puts the apple pie I brought over into the oven.

"I'm so sorry about dinner," Michelle says.

"You have nothing to be ashamed of." I squeeze her hand. "You forget, I didn't have a family like this growing up. It's wonderful to see how close you guys are, and how comfortable you are around each other. You should be proud of your family."

"I wish you had a better childhood." Her voice is low and soft, her eyes filled with sadness.

I lift a shoulder and let it fall. "It is what it is. I have Aiden now. I'm grateful for that. One day, I'll have my own kids, and maybe Aiden will too. Family isn't always about who you're related to by blood. It's about the people you choose to keep around, the ones who stick by your side."

"You're right," she says. "Speaking of family, have you heard from your private investigator about your sister?"

I shake my head. "He texted me and said it wasn't her."

"Does that happen a lot?"

"Yeah. It sucks. I'm draining my paychecks to keep looking for her, and to be honest, I don't even know what to do if I find her."

Michelle's eyebrows dip down. "You shouldn't waste your money on her. She chose to leave. Aiden is yours now."

I lift my thumb to smooth the lines between her eyebrows. "I love how passionate you are about the people you care about. It's my favorite thing about you."

Michelle's gaze drops to the ground. "Yeah, well, it's my least favorite thing about myself. Sometimes, I wish I could turn my emotions off altogether."

"Don't do that." I tip her chin up, my eyes pleading with her. "Your emotions are what makes you who you are. If you bury them, you're burying the incredible woman that I fell in love with." I swallow, taking a hesitant pause. "The woman I still—"

"Pie is ready!" Dan calls from the kitchen.

Michelle turns away and leaves me standing in the hallway.

The woman I still love.

MICHELLE

"You okay, Michy?"

I glance up at my father and muster a smile. "Yeah. Long day."

He nods, accepting my lie, though the look on his face tells me he knows better.

Michael drops onto the couch beside me, stretching his legs out across my lap.

"How're things with Angelina?" I ask.

A wide grin spreads his lips. "Fantastic."

"Someone got laid," Ryan singsongs from the recliner.

Michael flings a decorative pillow his way, pegging him in the head. "Don't be jealous."

My eyebrows lift. "You still haven't had sex with Jess?"

Ryan shakes his head. "She still wants to wait."

"The girl's got morals. I like her for you, Ry."

He rolls his eyes, but I catch the pleased smirk on his lips.

"Doesn't anyone want to ask about my sex life?" Caleb asks.

A simultaneous, "No," sounds from all four of us.

Caleb pouts. "Just because I'm the baby doesn't mean I *am* a baby, you know."

"It has nothing to do with your age," Michael says. "We just don't like your girl."

"Hey!" Caleb sits up and gestures to me. "Nobody likes Dick, but we all sit around and pretend. Why can't you do the same for me?"

"Because Michy is marrying Di—Richard," Dad says, catching himself. "You're just the idiot dating a girl who's been with half the football team. Big difference."

Caleb mutters something under his breath and stomps up the stairs.

Dad shakes his head. "God, I hope that kid doesn't come home with crabs."

We all laugh, but my smile is quick to fade.

I never thought I'd marry someone my family doesn't approve of. We're thick as thieves, a tight-knit group. Yet this is the one thing that drives us apart. It's why I've distanced myself from them.

"Start the wedding planning yet?" Dad asks.

I shake my head. "We're waiting to see if Richard makes partner at his firm."

"What does one thing have to do with the other?" Michael asks.

I explain Richard's logic to them, but it sounds even worse coming out of my mouth than it did when I'd heard it for the first time.

Michael's jaw flexes.

In my peripheral, I see Ryan shake his head.

Dad just stares at me with an unreadable expression.

And my patience finally snaps. "Okay, guys. Just fucking say it."

All three heads jerk back.

"What are you talking about, sweetheart?" Dad asks.

"You don't think I should marry Richard. Admit it."

He holds up his index finger. "Now, look. Nobody ever said we don't like him."

Ryan raises his hand. "I did. I said it."

Dad glares at him before returning his softened gaze to me. "To be honest, I don't know Richard enough to like him or dislike him. He's never around. I don't like that."

"I don't like it either." I drop my focus to my hands in my lap. "But it is what it is. That's his job. That's the life I chose."

Dad tilts his head. "That's the life *he* chose. You don't have to choose that same life for yourself. Not if you don't want it."

"Maybe you should ask yourself why you're choosing that life for yourself."

Our heads snap up to the stairs, where Caleb's sitting.

He shrugs at our shocked expressions. "What? I can be smart when I want to."

Dad chuckles. "Yes, you can." He pats the cushion next to him and Caleb drops down.

Michael scoots up to a seated position. "Caleb's right. You're choosing to be with someone who isn't right for you. Tonight, with Christopher and Aiden here, was the happiest I've seen you in a long time. You should be with someone who lifts you up. Richard is a dud. I don't know what you see in him."

"Mom wouldn't like him," Ryan says.

My eyes fill with tears as I look to Dad for confirmation on that.

He just shakes his head. "Mom would want you to follow your heart. Be with someone who lights you up, who will be a part of our family. If you think that person is Richard, then it's Richard. But if it's not ..." He trails off.

"Then dump his dick ass," Ryan finishes.

Caleb snorts. "Dick ass."

I leave Dad's house that night feeling even more confused than before.

I was on a sure and steady path before Christopher reentered my life. I need to do something to get myself back on track. Something that will take me in the right direction.

So when I get to Richard's apartment, I dial Raegan's number.

"Hey, Michelle."

"Hey, Rae. You busy?"

"Not at all. What's up?"

"Remember when you said you could help me with wedding planning?"

"Hell yes! What do you need? I'll be your wedding planner extraordinaire."

"I think it's time I start dress shopping."

15

MICHELLE

"Hello, do you have a reservation?"

Raegan steps forward with a bright smile. "Yes. We have an appointment with Shandra for two o'clock."

The woman's eyes scan down her iPad. "Ah, yes. Michelle. Right this way."

We're led through tall, ivory double-doors. Inside, different shades of white and cream gowns line the giant room. Satin, tulle, and lace swish around me. Two bride-to-be's stand on podiums in the center of the room, for all to see, their entourages smiling up at them from plush couches.

Instantly, my hands become clammy and my throat squeezes.

"Would you ladies care for some champagne?"

"Sure," Raegan says. Her smile fades when she turns to me. "You okay?"

I scratch an itch on my collar bone. "Yeah. Uh, could I have some water instead?"

"Of course." Then the lady disappears down a hallway.

With wide eyes, I make a slow turn to take it all in. "There are a lot of dresses here."

Raegan giggles. "It's overwhelming, I know."

"How do you pick one? Where do you even start?"

"Well, first," she says, removing my hand from my chest, "you stop scratching yourself. You tell the lady what kind of dress you're interested in, and then she pulls a bunch for you to try on. She'll help narrow it down."

"Kind of dress?" I echo.

"Like ball gowns, mermaids, trumpet, A-line ... oh, let's see. There are the different necklines. I think you'd look great in a sweetheart neckline. Then there are the shades of white, ivory, cream." She blinks expectantly. "You know. You just tell her which combinations you like."

A croaking sound leaves my throat. Luckily the receptionist returns with a glass of water, so I guzzle it down.

Raegan eyes me warily. "You sure you're okay?"

"I just don't know much about dresses. I'm not into all this," I wave my hand around the room, "girly shit."

"That's what I'm here for." A dark-haired woman smiles beside me. "I'm Evelyn, and I'll be helping you find your dream dress today."

I swallow past the dryness in my throat and force a smile.

"This is Michelle. I'm Raegan, the best friend." Raegan shakes the woman's hand.

Evelyn's eyes drag up and down my body. "You're tall and slender. Delicate bone structure. You've got a great collar bone."

"Uh, thanks?"

Her smile widens. "It's my job to notice the subtle features that will look great in a specific dress."

I shrug. "You can pick the dresses. I trust you."

Evelyn laughs. "I'll show you a few different styles, and you can tell me which one you like. That'll help us narrow down our selection. Before we start, is there a price range I should be aware of?"

"Nothing over two-thousand," Raegan answers for me.

We discussed it earlier in the car on the ride over. I had no clue how much wedding gowns go for. It seems ridiculous to spend so much on a dress you only wear once in your entire life.

Makes me wonder how much Mom spent on hers.

Makes me wish she were here so I could ask her.

Evelyn leads us to a spacious dressing room, and scurries off. Raegan and I take a seat on soft, velvet chairs.

Raegan lays her hand on my bouncing knee. "If you want to get out of here at any time, just say the word."

I shake my head. "I have to do this sooner or later. Might as well get it over with now."

Her worried expression tells me she doesn't like my response, but she keeps it to herself.

"Thanks for coming with me."

"Of course."

Evelyn's back within five minutes with four very different dresses. I scrunch my nose at the excessive poufiness of one of them.

Raegan giggles. "You might not like the way something looks on the hanger, but you won't know for sure until you try it on. It might surprise you."

"It would surprise me if there wasn't a family of four living underneath that one."

Evelyn throws her head back and laughs. "You remind me of myself when I was your age. I played basketball every day and lived in sweatpants."

My eyebrows shoot up. "Really?"

She nods. "Hard to believe, being that I'm working in a bridal shop now. I want to help girls like you feel like they don't have to conform. You don't have to be the stereotypical bride. But I also want to help you realize that you can wear a dress and still be your-self. You just have to find the right one."

My shoulders lower and the knot in my stomach begins to unravel. "Okay. Show us what you got."

Evelyn winks and turns to the first dress. "This one's the typical Cinderella ball gown. Not your style, I know, but let's just see what happens when you put it on. This next one is called a mermaid gown. You're tall, so I think this is a great option for you. This one here is an A-line. Strapless to show off your upper body."

I glance at each of them until she pulls the fourth dress out from behind the others. It's completely made of lace, no poof whatsoever, with delicate straps attached to what Raegan called a sweetheart neckline.

"This last one is my favorite for you. It's sexy and feminine, but simple, no frills. We'll put this one on last. Take your pick and try one on. I'll be just outside the door when you're ready. Give a holler if you need me."

Raegan squeals the second the door closes behind Evelyn. "Put this one on first." She shoves the giant ball gown at me and I stumble back against the wall.

"Shit, this thing weighs more than I do."

"Evelyn's right. You should try on some different styles to show you what you like and don't like. I know this is ridiculously poufy, but let's try it on for shits and giggles."

"Easy for you to say. You're not the one putting it on." I pause, examining the back of the dress. "Are all these buttons necessary?"

Raegan snatches the dress from my hands. "Give me that. I'll do it."

"Who thought that many buttons were a good idea? You're getting married, not jumping from an airplane."

Raegan lifts a brow. "Something tells me you'd be less nervous to jump out of a plane."

I hike a shoulder and plop back down onto the chair.

She's not wrong.

It takes Raegan way longer than it should to unbutton a damn dress. I step inside and wait while she takes the same amount of time to button it back up.

"How do you feel?" she asks.

"Like I was just swallowed by a giant humpback whale."

I catch her smirk in the mirror.

"Come on. Look at me. I look ridiculous."

"Just go outside and show Evelyn."

"Oh, no. I'm not walking out there and standing in the middle of the entire store."

A soft knock on the door prompts Raegan to crack it open.

Evelyn sticks her head through and her eyes slide up and down my body. Then she shakes her head. "Nope. Try the next one."

Relieved, I try the mermaid-style dress next. My knees are forced together, and I have to take baby steps in order to shuffle toward the mirror.

"How do people move in these things? No wonder Ariel wanted legs."

"Looks great on you, though," Raegan says. "I'm too short to ever wear anything like that."

I rest my elbow on her shoulder. "You're not short. You're fun-sized."

We laugh as I step out of the dress and try on the next. The A-line does nothing for me, so we don't bother showing Evelyn.

"Last one," Raegan says as I slip into the lace dress.

There's a zipper on this one, with fake buttons concealing it on the outside, so it's easy to put on. It fits me like a glove, the lace hugging my modest curves. The bottom of the skirt flares out, allowing me to move freely, and the straps on my shoulders are just enough to hold the dress in place. My B-cups even look a little fuller with the sweetheart neckline.

"Wow," Raegan says on an exhale. "You look incredible."

She pulls open the door and waves Evelyn over.

Evelyn smiles. "I knew that dress would work. Come on." She tugs my wrist. "I have a better mirror."

I pull back. "Please. I don't want to stand up in front of everyone out there."

"We won't. I promise."

I follow her with Raegan beside me. At the end of the hall, there's a small podium for me to stand on in front of a tri-fold mirror. There are women walking in and out of dressing rooms, but no one's focus is on me. It's private.

"What's your shoe size?" Evelyn asks.

"Eight."

She nods. "Be right back."

Raegan pulls the hair tie out of my pony tail, and my hair cascades down around my shoulders. I glare at her, but she smiles. "I just want you to get the full effect." She smacks my ass. "Now get up there and see how gorgeous you look."

Evelyn re-enters the hallway with a pair of strappy heels and a veil in her hands.

Small beads of sweat form on the back of my neck.

Evelyn bends down to guide my feet into the shoes. Then, she takes my hand and helps me step up onto the podium. She moves behind me and secures the veil in my hair.

Raegan covers her mouth with her fingertips as she stares up at me.

My eyes roam over my form in the mirror.

You look like your mother.

That's when I remember: Mom wore a long-sleeve lace dress on the day she married my father. There's a picture of them hanging on the wall in the hallway at my Dad's, and I always used to stare at it when I was a little girl. Mom looked so beautiful, so elegant.

And she looked happy.

I'd always wanted to look like her on my wedding day.

You can wear the same dress, but will you look as happy standing next to Richard?

In an instant, Christopher flashes through my mind ...

I can see him, standing at the altar in a beautiful church, looking as handsome as ever in a black tux. His warm hazel eyes are on me, glossing over the closer I get. Aiden's beside him, that goofy sideways grin on his adorable face. My father beams beside me, proudly walking me down the aisle. My brothers are there too, strong and confident, excited to gain another brother. My heart beats fast, but I'm not nervous. How could I be? It's him.

It's always been him.

Tears sting my eyes, and my airway feels restricted. I try to take a deep breath, but there's a heavy weight sitting on my chest.

You can't marry Richard.

My skin heats, the flush spreading across my chest and up my neck. My arms feel itchy, and I start to scratch at them.

Raegan's at my side, but I can barely make out what she's saying.

"I can't ... I need ... I ..." Words won't come out as I struggle to suck in air.

You can't marry Richard.

The room starts to spin around me.

Evelyn helps Raegan guide me down from the podium, ushering me back into the dressing room. They make quick work of the zipper, and once I'm out of the dress, I sink down onto the chair.

"Put your head between your knees," Evelyn says. "Breathe in through your nose and out your mouth."

You can't marry Richard.

Raegan kneels on the floor beside me, rubbing my back in small circles. "It's okay, Michelle."

You can't marry Richard.

"Just breathe."

You can't marry Richard.

"Everything's gonna be okay."

You can't marry Richard.

I sit up slowly, running my hands over my face. Evelyn hands me a glass of water, and I let the cool liquid slide down my throat, soothing the fire in my chest.

Raegan's emerald eyes are wide as she stares up at me, her hand gripping my knee. "Talk to me. What's going on?"

I glance up to Evelyn, and back down to Raegan. I square my shoulders and cover her hand with mine.

"I can't marry Richard."

* * *

My hands shake when I hear the key in the door.

Take deep breaths. You got this.

My heart pounds in time with the sounds of Richard's shoes on the laminate.

"Hey, babe." He enters the kitchen and dips down to kiss my temple.

"How was your day?"

"Long and exhausting."

"Dinner's ready for you."

He nods and plops down into his chair at the table. "Smells good."

I needed to keep busy today. I cooked everything I had in the fridge. I just didn't have the stomach to eat any of it.

Richard makes himself a plate and digs in. He recounts the events of his cases today, but I can't hear a word over the blood pounding in my ears.

"Michelle?"

My head snaps up to look at him. "Yeah?"

"I asked if you're okay. You haven't touched the food."

I try to swallow past the dry lump in my throat, but it doesn't work. I gulp my water and smack the cup down onto the table. "We need to talk."

Richard pushes his plate away, leaning back and folding his hands in his lap. "Okay ..."

With a shaky breath and a heavy heart, I force myself to look him in his eyes. "I don't think I can do this anymore."

His eyebrows pull together. "Do what?"

"This." I gesture between us. "Us. I can't ... I can't be with you."

"Where is this coming from?"

"I know it seems like it's out of the blue, and I guess for you it is, but for me it's been building for a while. You've been working these long hours, and I can't sit here alone every day. I know you're working hard to make partner at your firm, and I couldn't be more proud of you for that. You have this incredible drive and you're full of ambition. It's one of the things I love about you.

"But the more I think about our future, about starting a family, the worse I feel. We can't even plan our wedding because of your schedule. How are we going to raise children if you're always putting work first?"

He nods, quiet for a moment, letting my words sink in. "So this is about my job?"

I could lie. I could say yes and blame everything on his job.

It'd be the easy way out.

Keep going.

My gaze drops to my lap. "No. It's not just about your job."

He releases a sigh. "I thought as much."

"What do you mean?"

Richard leans forward and takes my hand in his. "We don't want the same things in life. I don't think I can give you the kind of life you want. And you shouldn't have to compromise who you are just to be with me. It's not fair to either of us."

Tears threaten to brim over my lids, but I hold them back. Not yet. Not now. "I'm sorry."

He shakes his head. "It's not your fault."

"You're not mad at me?"

He offers me a sad smile, lifting his fingers to my cheek. "No, babe. I could never be mad at you."

A tear rolls down my cheek. "I'll pack up my things tonight. I can take the day off tomorrow and be out by the time you get home."

"No. You can have the apartment. I'll find another."

"No." I shake my head. "This is your apartment. I'll stay at my Dad's until I can find another place."

"Are you sure?"

I nod. "I need to go home for a while. Figure things out."

Then I slip the engagement ring off my finger and hold it out to him. "You can get your money back."

"I don't care about the money," he says, shaking his head.

I place it in the palm of his hand, curling his fingers around it. "I don't deserve this. It's yours."

He heaves a sigh, looking down at the glistening ring in his hand. "Can I give you a piece of advice?"

I lift a brow. "Sure."

"Listen to what your heart is telling you, and don't be afraid to go after it."

A smile tugs at the corner of my mouth. "That's really great advice."

He shrugs. "I'm a good lawyer."

A laugh bubbles up and escapes me, while tears drop down my cheeks. "That is true."

Richard spends the rest of the night working in his office while I pack my clothes into my suitcase.

I just called off my wedding, broke up with my fiancé, and I'll be moving back home with my family. I should be devastated.

But I'm not.

I'm relieved.

A weight has been lifted off my shoulders, because I realized something after my conversation with Richard:

Everyone was wrong. Richard is *not* a dick. And it's not that he didn't make me happy. I wasn't making *myself* happy. My own happiness is up to *me*. No one else can be responsible for creating it.

No one else but me.

The other night at my father's house, Christopher told me not to bury my emotions because they are what make me who I am. Who I've always been. For too long, I've tried to be someone I'm not. I've let myself believe that I don't need emotions because they only lead you to pain. I let heartbreak and fear dictate who I should be. I've settled for less than what I wanted because I thought it was the only way. The only choice.

I destroyed my own happiness out of fear.

But I can't be that person anymore.

It's time to get back to being who you really are, my inner voice whispers.

It's time to get back to you.

16

CHRISTOPHER

Michelle isn't at work on Monday morning.

I shoot her a text on my lunch break, pretending to care about tutoring when I really just want to make sure she's okay.

Me: WE STILL ON FOR TUTORING TONIGHT?

    Michelle: Yes, why wouldn't we be?

    Me: You're not at work. Thought you might be sick.

    Michelle: Took a mental health day.

    Me: Everything good?

    Michelle: I'll be back tomorrow.

    Me: That doesn't answer my question.

    Michelle: I'm fine Christopher. See you later.

UNEASE TWISTS MY GUT ALL AFTERNOON. IT MUST BE WRITTEN ALL over my face because when Raegan brings her class to the gym later, she hangs back and waits for the kids to take their spots inside.

"You okay?"

I nod. "I'm fine."

"Then why do you look like someone died?"

"I'm worried about Michelle. She's not in today."

She hikes a shoulder. "Maybe she's sick."

"I texted her but she seemed ... off."

Raegan chews on the inside of her cheek. "Okay, look. If I tell you something, will you swear not to tell her I told you?"

My eyebrows dip down. "You know what's wrong?"

She nods. "But you have to swear not to tell her, Chris."

I turn to the students waiting for instructions. "Free play today, guys."

Raegan's class cheers.

"Sarah, Joshua, and Peyton, come get the scooters and hula hoops. Tommy and Sebastian, you guys can get the basketballs."

The kids pick their stations and I turn up the music. Then I focus all my attention on Raegan. "I swear I won't say anything. Just tell me what's going on."

Raegan runs her fingers through her hair. "I shouldn't be saying anything to you. I shouldn't get in the middle of this."

"But you were my friend before you were hers, so you have to tell me out of obligation."

Her head jerks back. "Are you pulling the seniority card on our friendship right now?"

"You're damn right I am. Now speak, woman."

"Michelle broke up with Richard this weekend," she blurts out.

My jaw falls open and my eyes widen in shock.

What? She broke up with him?

"What happened?" I ask.

"I took her wedding dress shopping on Sunday. She was nervous, but that's normal. Then she freaked out." Raegan shakes her head. "I think she had a panic attack."

My heartrate spikes, adrenaline pulsing through me. "Why?"

"Between me and you, I don't think she ever wanted to marry that guy. I don't know him, but she didn't seem happy with him."

"So she's not with Dick anymore?"

"No, Chris. She's not with Dick anymore."

"I have to see her."

"No!" Her green eyes widen. "Christopher Hastings, you cannot tell Michelle that I told you. You have to pretend like you don't know. Let her tell you in her own time."

I nod like a zombie. "In her own time."

"Yes. She'll tell you when she's ready."

"When she's ready."

"Why are you repeating everything I'm saying?"

"I don't know," I murmur. "I just can't believe she broke up with him. Do you think ... do you think maybe it's ..."

"Because of you?" she finishes. "I don't know. But I think you being here might've had something to do with it."

Michelle broke up with Dick.

She's not marrying him.

She's *single*.

I know I can't assume that this means anything will change between us, but damnit if I can't help my dumb, hopeful heart from getting carried away.

Raegan pats me on the shoulder. "I'm rooting for you, my friend. Just give her some time."

Time.

It's been five years.

What's a little longer, right?

MICHELLE

Dad answers the door with a smile on his face.

"To what do I owe this surprise?" Then his eyes fall to my suitcase and multiple bags lined up on the porch.

"Oh, honey." He swings open the door and I step into his outstretched arms.

"Think I can have my old room back for a while, Dad?"

"Of course you can. It's yours for as long as you need it." He releases me and leans onto the bannister, craning his neck up the staircase. "Boys! Come help your sister carry her bags inside."

Thunder sounds as they race to the stairs. Caleb is the first one down, but Ryan shoves past him and almost goes through the screen door in the process.

Michael shakes his head, rubbing the sleep from his eyes. He must've worked a nightshift at the hospital last night. "What's going on? What bags are we carrying in?"

Ryan sticks his head through the front door. "Shit, Michy. Are you moving back home?"

I nod.

"Ding, dong, the dick is gone!" Caleb sings.

145

He and Ryan lock elbows and spin around the porch, dancing to Caleb's new song.

Dad shakes his head. "Get your asses inside! The neighbors don't need to wake up and see your dicks flopping around in your boxers."

And just like that, I'm home.

After Caleb and Ryan leave for school, I plop onto the couch in between Dad and Michael.

"So how did he take it?" Michael asks.

I arch a brow. "How do you know he didn't break up with me?"

Michael laughs. "'Cuz I know."

I roll my eyes. "He took it fine."

"Knew it."

"It went better than I expected actually. He told me to follow my heart. Said he'd leave me the apartment, the ring." I wave my hand around. "Everything."

Dad's eyebrows shoot up. "Guess he's not such a dick after all."

Michael and I crack up laughing, and it feels good. Like my soul is shaking off the dust and remembering what it's like to be happy again.

"He really wasn't a bad guy," I say.

Dad nods. "Just not *your* guy."

"You tell Christopher?" Michael asks, side-eyeing me.

"No. Why would I tell him?"

He and Dad exchange glances.

"Okay, what the hell was that?"

"What?" Dad asks innocently.

"That look you guys gave each other. I saw that."

"I mean, it's no secret the boy is in love with you." Dad shrugs, like it's common knowledge.

My nostrils flare as I shoot daggers through my eyeballs at Michael. "I told you not to tell anyone."

Michael's hands fly up in front of him. "I didn't tell him anything!"

I flick my eyes to Dad.

Dad sighs. "Michy, with the way Christopher was looking at you

146

from across that dinner table, I'd say Helen Keller herself could've seen how much that boy cares for you. Your brother didn't have to tell me anything."

Michael gives me a smug smile, crossing his arms over his chest.

Michael didn't tell him. You just did, you idiot.

I groan, face-planting into my palms.

"The question is," Dad continues, "do you love him?"

I mumble against my hands.

"What was that? Couldn't hear ya," Michael yells.

I sit upright and flatten my hair with my hands. "I said I don't know."

Dad leans over and squeezes my knee. "I'm gonna need the full story here, kid. It's the only way I'll be able to help you with my magical dad powers."

I giggle and rest my head on his shoulder. "Well, Christopher and I dated for a few months in college. We were in love. And then one night he disappeared and I never heard from him again." I crane my neck to look up at him. "Can your dad powers fix that?"

Dad's quiet a moment. "He had to leave to take care of Aiden."

Michael's eyes go wide. "Oh, shit! That's why he left you!"

I shake my head. "Mikey, I love you, but you're an idiot."

Dad nods in agreement. "Took me two seconds to connect those dots."

Michael flips us off. "What happened?"

"His junkie sister dumped him and left. Christopher said he didn't want me to drop out of college and go with him. Said it'd be better if I didn't know."

"You hate that," Dad says. "When people make decisions for you without consulting you first."

I sit up straight, anger running through me now. "Who is he to say what's best for me? How could he just disappear like that and not tell me? Why would he think I was better off without him?"

"He's right, you know."

My head jerks back. "Are you kidding me, Dad?"

"When you love someone, truly love someone, you put them first. You sacrifice every selfish need you have for the sake of her well-being. It doesn't matter how badly you want something. What matters is doing what's best for her."

"How is breaking my heart into a million little pieces, leaving me to be tortured by questions *for years*, doing what's best for me?"

"You needed to finish college and get your degree," Michael says. "He was looking out for your future."

"I wanted my future to be with *him*! I could've gotten my degree anywhere. I would've helped them. We could've come back here, together. Aiden would've had a family. *That's* what love is about: Getting through the hard times *together*. Not leaving and going it alone!"

My chest is heaving, tears streaming down my face.

Dad wraps his arms around me and pulls me into a hug. My sobs become louder in the safety of his embrace, racking through my body like shockwaves. I haven't let myself cry like this in years, the dam finally breaking.

Dad rocks me back and forth, stroking my hair. "It's okay, my Michy. Let it all out."

I don't know how long it takes, but we remain this way until the tears dry up, and my breaths come easier. And once again, it feels like another piece of myself has returned.

I lean back, wiping my nose on the back of my sleeve.

Michael hands me a box of Kleenex. "Well, I guess that answers Dad's question."

"What do you mean?"

"You still love him, Mich."

"How can I love someone who hurt me so bad? How can I trust him? What if something else happens, and he tries to make a decision for me again?" I shake my head. "I don't know if I can take that chance."

"Unfortunately, that's the way love goes," Dad says. "There's no guarantee that your partner won't hurt you. But it's worth it. Love is worth all of the risk. I lost your mother way before I ever thought I would. But if I had the chance to do it over again? I'd still choose her. I'd still marry her. Losing her too soon doesn't outweigh the possibility of never having known her in the first place."

148

I stare at my father in disbelief. "You'd still be with her knowing the amount of pain you'd feel when you lost her?"

"Absolutely."

Michael swipes a tear from his cheek. "Having something for a little while is better than not ever having it at all."

Is it though?

That question plagues my mind for the remainder of the day.

CHRISTOPHER

I don't know how I'm going to keep my promise to Raegan.

Michelle's only been here for five minutes and already I'm about to burst.

I haven't even told Aiden. The kid would get too excited and assume the wrong thing. I don't want to get his hopes up. My own damn hopes are up. That's enough false hope for one house.

"Oh my God, Aiden! That's fantastic!"

I rush over to the table. "What's fantastic?"

Aiden's cheeks are red. "I wwwanted to wwwait until Mmmichelle got here to show yyyou." He holds up his math test. "I got 100% on my test."

I lean over and slap my hand against Aiden's. "That's great, bud. This is definitely going on the fridge."

"It's all because of mmmy tutor," he says, blushing an even deeper shade of red.

"No, no," Michelle says, waving her hands. "It's because of your hard work and determination to learn."

"Spoken like a true teacher." I nudge her with my shoulder. "This calls for a celebration. What would you like as your reward, bud?"

Aiden scrunches his nose. "Can I thinnnk about it and get back to yyyou?"

"Of course. Let's order pizza for dinner. Whaddya say, Bambi? Will you stay?"

"Sure. How can I turn down pizza?"

I roll my eyes. "Sure. We'll pretend it's the pizza that's making you stay."

She giggles and my heart skips a beat at the sound.

"Wwwhy does he call yyyou Bambi?" Aiden asks.

Michelle clears her throat, fidgeting in her seat. I know talking about her mom makes her uncomfortable, but she surprises me by telling Aiden the story.

"My mom always used to call me Bambi. She said I had these big, brown doe eyes when I was a kid. Too big for my head. Took me a while to grow into them." She smiles before it fades. "When she died, I really felt like I *was* Bambi."

I cover Michelle's hand with mine, trying to ignore the glaring bare space on her ring finger.

"When we dated in college, your uncle called me doe eyes. He hadn't known that was my nickname growing up, until I told him."

I fixate on our joined hands. "We always wondered if our moms brought us together, all the way from heaven."

Aiden nods, taking it all in. "Well, then my mom brought us all together too."

Michelle rests her head on his shoulder. "Do you ever think about your mom?"

I hold my breath waiting for his response.

"Sommmetimes," he says. "Like on Mmmother's Day, or on mmmy birthday. I'll see a TV show and wwwonder what it'd be like to have a mmmom. A good onnne, like yyyou guys had." He shrugs. "But it doesn't rrreally mmmatter if I have one or nnnot."

"Why do you say?" she asks.

His eyes lift to meet mine. "Because I have all I'll ever nnneed wwwith Uncle Chris."

Tears blur my vision. Those ten words are the most important words Aiden could've ever said.

"Yeah, you do," Michelle agrees, her eyes glossy as she looks up at me. "You lucked out with this one."

I give her hand a squeeze and turn around before any tears escape. "I'll go order the pizza now."

* * *

Michelle stays later than usual after we finish dinner.

She's curled up on the couch, staring at the blank TV screen.

"You know, it works better if you turn it on," I say, sitting beside her.

She chuckles. "Sorry, I was thinking."

"Anything you want to talk about?"

Like, say, the fact that you're not with Richard anymore.

"Have you ever thought about decorating this place?"

I look around at the bare, stained walls. "I didn't think I'd be here long enough, to be honest. But the rent is cheap and this is what I can afford right now."

"Maybe we can spruce it up a little. For the time being."

"We? As in, you want to help?"

She shrugs. "Sure. Some paint, a few pictures on the wall. Nothing crazy."

I push off the couch and hold my hand out for hers. "Come with me. I want to show you something."

Michelle takes my hand as I lead her into the hallway, and inside my bedroom.

I flip the light on and watch as Michelle's eyes bounce around the bare walls.

I crouch down in front of my closet, reaching into the back, and coming out with an old shoebox. Then I sit on one corner of my bed, and pat the space next to me.

Michelle lowers herself beside the box, peering at it curiously.

"I might not decorate the walls with pictures, but that doesn't mean I don't have them." I lift the lid and set it onto the comforter, revealing a stack of pictures. "Some are of my mom, some are my baby pictures. I have a few of Aiden, ones I took from my dad's before we left. And a bunch are of me and you."

Her lips part as she takes the photos from me, sifting through them. "You took these with you before you left?"

I nod.

A smile spreads across her face when she holds up a picture. "Do you remember this? The bowling ball got stuck to your thumb and you had to ice your hand until it came out."

"Not the best impression on a first date."

She giggles. "Oh, you left an impression." She holds up another photo. "This was such a great concert!"

"Yeah, until that mosh pit started and somebody knocked my glasses off my face."

"It was always an adventure with you." Her smile slips. "I haven't done something fun like that in so long."

I'm about to suggest going to a concert when Michelle's hands fly to her mouth as she gasps. "Is that ... oh my God ... Chris."

With wide eyes, she reaches into the box and pulls out a red pool ball. "Is this the ball you hit me with the night we met?"

I nod, rubbing the back of my neck nervously.

"How did you get this? I was with you all night."

"I swiped it off the floor when I was on my way over to apologize to you. Slipped it into my pocket once we started talking. Holding onto all of these memories gave me hope, like maybe one day our paths would cross again. I didn't want to believe that our story was over."

"It shouldn't have been," she says quietly. "I've been angry with you for a long time, you know."

My eyes tighten. "I know. I'm sorry I hurt you. Every night, I think about how differently things might've turned out had I made a different choice."

"You could've told me. We could've figured it out together." Her lips pull into a frown. "I think that's what upset me the most, that you didn't even give me a choice."

I take both of her hands in mine, dipping my head down so she looks me in my eyes. "I'm sorry, Michelle. I'm so, so sorry. I thought

I was doing the right thing. What kind of person would I be if I let you drop out of college and throw away your dream of becoming a teacher? I didn't know what would happen once I got to Tennessee, if I could raise a kid on my own."

She offers me a small smile. "Look how good that kid turned out."

I huff out a laugh. "Yeah, he is pretty great."

We stare into each other's eyes, her hands still clasped in mine.

"Michelle, I've never stopped loving you. Not once has my heart wavered. And seeing you now, seeing the incredible woman that you've become, I'm enamored by you. My heart swells when you walk into a room, just the same as it did when we were dating.

"I believe that we were meant to be together. Meeting you at that frat party was fate. And I know we took a detour for a while, because of me, but you're sitting here in front of me right now, and I know in my heart that there's a reason the universe brought you back to me."

I don't know where I'm going with this. I don't have a plan. The words are flowing from my heart because I need her to know. I need her to hear everything I've been wanting to say, all this time.

I tuck a strand of her hair behind her ear and let my fingers linger on her cheek, caressing her soft skin. "I still love you, Michelle. And I always will."

Her bottom lip trembles, and her watery eyes look into mine for what feels like forever.

Come on, Bambi. Give me something.

"I forgive you for what you did," she says with a shaky voice. "I understand why you left, and why you didn't want me to know. I get it all, and I forgive you."

My heart thunders in its cage. "You don't know how long I've dreamed of hearing those words."

She slips her hands out of mine. "I should go. It's getting late."

I stand with her, wishing I could say something, do something to make her stay. To make her say that she loves me to, that we can finally be together now.

But I know I have to let her go.

She needs time.

So I walk her out and say goodnight.

I'm straightening up in the kitchen when my phone buzzes with a missed call alert on the counter.

My stomach drops when I see that it's from Phil.

I press the phone to my ear, praying he picks up.

"Hey, kid," he answers. "Wasn't sure if you were still up."

"Sorry, I didn't have my phone on me. What's up?"

"I found your sister."

My mouth goes dry in an instant. "You found her?"

"Yep. She's two hours away from your old house."

"Is she ... is she still on drugs?"

"I can't say for sure yet. Wanted to let you know as soon as I could. She's living in a trailer park."

"Now what?" I ask more to myself than to Phil.

"That's up to you. If you want, I can give you her whereabouts and you can come see her for yourself."

"I'm not ready to make a trip down there yet. Is it possible for you to get her number for me?"

"Anything's possible, kid. I'll keep you posted."

The call ends, but I remain standing in the middle of the kitchen with my phone pressed to my ear.

Phil found my sister.

He finally found her.

Now what?

MICHELLE

For years, I've wondered where Christopher was. Especially during the holidays.

Who was he eating turkey with on Thanksgiving?

Did he have anyone to buy gifts for on Christmas?

Who was he kissing when the ball dropped on New Year's Eve?

Today, after all this time, I know where he is on Thanksgiving, and where he'll be for Christmas.

Jury's still out on who he'll be kissing on New Year's though.

Christopher's eyes meet mine across the table at my dad's house, and he smiles. He and Aiden fit right in here. I want to tell him that. I want to tell him that I'm not with Richard anymore. I want to tell him that I ...

Well, I'm not sure *what* I want to tell him.

Instead, I try to convey everything through a look, hoping he can hear the unspoken words that hang between us.

Aiden and Caleb are talking about movies; Ryan and Michael have their girlfriends by their sides, looking happy as ever; and Dad watches us from the head of the table. I know his heart is full, having all of us together like this.

He and Christopher get along well. So well that I had to excuse myself from a thirty minute conversation about the game of chess earlier.

Chess.

I mean, who even talks about chess? Whenever I see people playing it, they're just staring at the board in complete silence like they're watching paint dry. What is there to talk about?

Regardless, I love seeing them together.

I love having Christopher here.

Seeing the box of our pictures in his room the other night hit me hard—as hard as that fated red pool ball hit me five years ago.

All I've wanted was to forget about him, forget about every single one of those moments we shared. It was easier to bury the pain. Cover it up with anger.

Meanwhile, Christopher left everything he'd ever wanted behind to take care of his nephew and he doesn't resent it. He doesn't let it bring him down. It's not who he is. He couldn't harbor a bad feeling if he tried.

The more I'm with him, the more I'm reminded of why I fell so hard for him in the first place. He's got a heart of gold and it shines onto everyone. He's everything that's pure and good in this world, and he deserves it in return.

My feelings are rising to the surface, making their way up through the cracks in the darkness I've been living in.

Maybe it's time I told him about my break-up.

Maybe it's time I told him how I'm feeling.

Maybe I'll tell him tonight.

* * *

"THANKS FOR INVITING US."

"I'm glad you came." I twist on my bed to face Christopher. "Is everything okay? You seem like something's on your mind."

He picks at a thread sticking out of the armrest. "You were always good at reading me."

"You're an easy read." I lift my thumb and rub it in between his furrowed brows. "Talk to me."

Christopher heaves a sigh and lifts his eyes to mine. "The P.I. found my sister."

My spine stiffens. "Oh. Really? In Tennessee?"

"Yeah. In a trailer park a few hours from my dad's house. The P.I. called a few nights ago. He got her number for me so I can contact her." His eyes drop to his lap. "If I want to."

"What are you going to do?"

He shrugs. "I don't know. I'm torn."

I chew on my bottom lip. "Does Aiden know?"

"No. I don't want to tell him until I find out if she's clean."

"What if she is? What difference does it make?"

Christopher runs his fingers through his hair, blowing a stream of air through his lips. "The kid deserves to know his mother. If she's clean, maybe she's looking for him. Maybe she wants to make things right."

My head snaps back. "How could she make things right, exactly? By taking him back to Tennessee? By taking him away from you, his school, and his friends?"

"I don't know, okay? I don't know what would happen."

"It's simple. Aiden is a minor. If she wants him back, she has the legal power to do so. She can take him away from you just like that," I say, snapping my fingers.

He scrubs a hand over his face. "And what if he wants to go?"

"Well, you won't know until you ask him." I lean forward, forcing his gaze to meet mine. "You need to tell him, Chris. Let him make the choice. Don't take that away from him like ..." I bite my tongue, shaking my head.

"Like I did to you," he finishes.

"I'm just saying, he has a right to know. He should be a part of the decision."

"He's a kid. He can't make important decisions like this."

"He's old enough to handle it. And I wasn't a kid, yet you made the decision for me."

"This isn't about you, Michelle. You say you forgive me, but you keep throwing it in my face every chance you get!"

159

"I'm only bringing it up because it's true. This is what you do. You think you know what's best for people, but you don't!"

Christopher's lips press into a firm line, and the mattress shakes as he pushes to his feet. "Thanks for having us over for dinner. I'm gonna call it a night."

"Chris, wait." I stride into the hallway after him.

He knocks on Ryan and Caleb's door. "Aiden, it's time to go."

"Can't wwwe stay a little longerrr?"

"Now, Aiden."

I meet Aiden's concerned gaze in the hallway and muster the best smile I can, wrapping him in a hug. "Your uncle's really tired. You can come back tomorrow and play with the boys."

He follows Christopher downstairs and out the front door.

This is *so* not how I thought this night would end.

CHRISTOPHER

That was *not* how I imagined Thanksgiving ending.

I know Michelle is worried that my sister will want to take Aiden away. I'm worried about that too. But I can't make a decision out of selfishness. I have to do the right thing, for Aiden's sake.

Is this really the right thing though?

Before I can talk myself out of it, I press the green call button and take a deep breath.

Here we go.

"Hello?" My sister's voice rasps through the speaker.

"H-hey, Cindy. It's Christopher."

"Christopher?"

"Your brother."

It's silent on the line, save for the blood pounding in my ears.

"Shit," she mutters. "Dad's dead, ain't he?"

"What? No. I mean, I don't think he is."

"He sick or somethin'?"

"Not that I'm aware of. Haven't spoken to him in a few years."

Her husky laugh takes me by surprise. "Well, I'll be damned. You're about the last person I'd ever expect to hear from."

"Yeah. You're the last person I thought I'd ever call."

"So if dad ain't sick or dying, why you callin' me?"

I scrub my hand over my jaw, sucking in a breath. "I'm calling ... I'm calling you about your son."

"What about him?"

"I ... I ... are you still using, Cindy?"

"Been clean for eight months now. Not that that's any of your damn business."

"Eight months. That's good. You working?"

"What are you writing a god damn autobiography on me or some shit?"

"Well, no. An autobiography is something someone writes about themselves. I'd be writing a biography if—"

"Cut to the chase, baby bro. I got shit to do and you're wastin' my time."

I swallow. "Right. Okay, then. I'm calling to see if you're interested in getting to know your son. If you've been wondering where he is, or if you'd want to see him."

"What's the boy causin' you trouble? You can beat his ass if he ain't actin' right."

My head jerks back. "What? No. He's no trouble at all. I just—"

"You tryin' to give him back? Cuz I ain't interested. I got my own life. My own problems to worry about."

"He ... he *is* your life. He's your son."

"Look, Chris. If you don't want him anymore, then just give him up. There's plenty of rich white bitches out there lookin' for a retard to raise."

My mouth falls open in horror. "Are you kidding me?"

"Why do you think I left his ass at Dad's house? I can't be bothered takin' care of someone fucked up like that. You hear the way he speaks? You can't tell me that's normal. Should've aborted him like I wanted to in the first place."

The rage that has been simmering in the pit of my stomach roars to a boil. "You selfish, junkie piece of shit!"

She laughs but gets cut off by her smoker's cough. "If you like him so much, why are you callin' me? You think I owe you somethin' cuz you took care of him?"

"I'm not looking for money," I grit out. "I just thought ... you know what? It doesn't matter what I thought. Aiden doesn't deserve you. And you don't deserve to know him."

"You think you're better than me? Why, because you got that fancy college degree? You livin' in a house now, thinkin' you're a big man? Don't forget where you came from. You can change your clothes but you'll always be trash like me. Like Dad."

"I'll *never* be like you. You can go back to your pathetic fucking waste of a life and forget I ever called."

"Gladly."

She ends the call before I can say another word.

I toss my phone onto my mattress and pace the room, seething.

"God damnit!" My fist shoots out and I punch through the sheetrock in the wall next to my door.

That woman will *never* get near Aiden. She won't get to know him, or watch him grow up, or see his precious smile.

I'll make sure of it.

He belongs to me and that's all he needs.

Aiden is *mine*.

MICHELLE

M y phone buzzes for the third time this morning.
"Now he wants to talk?" I mutter, ignoring the call.

I'd tried contacting Christopher several times after our fight last night. Tried to apologize. But he sent my calls straight to voicemail.

Now, he can see what it feels like to be ignored.

My phone buzzes again, this time Raegan's number lighting up the screen.

"Morning, Rae. What's—"

"Where have you been?"

"Right here. In my bed."

"Christopher has been trying to get in touch with you! Why aren't you answering?"

I roll my eyes. "Great, he's using you as the middle man now."

"Michelle, Aiden's gone."

My head jerks off the pillow. "What do you mean gone?"

"Chris woke up this morning and Aiden wasn't in his bed. He left a note on his desk. He ran away."

What?

My heart stalls out, knees go weak. I grasp the edge of my mattress for support. "How can he ... why would he run away?"

"I don't know. But we need to go help Chris find Aiden."

My heart is in my throat as I leap out of bed. "I'm getting dressed now."

I throw on sweatpants and a hoodie. Running down the hallway, I call Christopher. He answers on the first ring.

"Michelle." His voice is strained. He's panicking.

"I'm on my way."

"He left, Michelle. His duffle bag is missing too."

"What did his note say?"

"He overheard part of my phone call to my sister last night. He thinks I want to take him back to her."

I push through my front door and dart into the driveway. "You spoke to your sister?"

"Yes. You were right, Michelle. She's a piece of shit." A strained sob escapes him. "You were right. I should've listened to you."

I swing myself into my car and turn the key in the ignition, ripping my seatbelt over my shoulder. "Don't worry about that now. Let's focus on finding Aiden. Where have you checked already?"

"I called Jordan's parents and two of the nearby hospitals."

"Okay, we need to split up so we can cover more ground. Raegan will check the mall. You go to the train station. We don't know what time he left, but he's a young kid on crutches, so he couldn't have gotten very far."

"Where will you go?"

"I'll figure it out. I'll call Michael at the hospital. Dad, Ryan, and Caleb can help too. The more help we have, the better."

Christopher lets out a heavy sigh. "Michelle, I don't know what I'll do if—"

"Don't. Everything's going to be fine. Keep your head up and keep looking for him. We're going to find him."

After a few phone calls, Dad, Caleb, and Ryan are on the lookout for Aiden.

Michael said he'll let me know if Aiden turns up in the Emergency Room.

For the next hour, I check all the local places: Diners, restaurants, coffee shops. I've asked dozens of strangers, "Have you seen this boy?" to no avail.

I'm driving when a thought hits me.

I think I know where he is.

I swerve around the median and gun it in the opposite direction. "Please be where I think you are."

* * *

I SWING MY CAR DOOR SHUT AND JOG ACROSS THE STREET.

Come on, Aiden.

The temperature here is about ten degrees cooler, the constant breeze whipping my hair into my face. I zip my jacket higher to cover my neck and pull my hood up. Several dedicated runners clomp past me as I make my way across the wooden planks.

My eyes scan the desolate boardwalk. There's no sign of him.

When I get to the arcade, I spot him through the glass door.

His thin body, crutches resting on the machine beside him, that messy mop of hair. Relief floods through me.

I slip inside and quietly take the seat next to him, watching him as his eyes follow his car on the track of the digital screen.

"Hey."

He doesn't turn to look at me. "Hey."

"You know, if you wanted to come to the arcade, you could've called me."

His eyes remain fixed on the screen.

"What's going on, Cap'? Talk to me."

"Did yyyou know?"

"Did I know what?"

His hands drop from the steering wheel and he gives me a hard stare. "Did yyyou know?"

I heave a sigh, running my fingers through my hair. "Did I know that your uncle hired a private investigator to find your mother? Yes."

His lips press into a line. "Did yyyou know he wwwanted to give mmme back to her?"

166

My eyes narrow. "What are you talking about?"

"I heard him. Last nnnight on the phonnne. He said he wwwants mmmy mmmother to get to know mmme. He asked her if she wwwants to see mmme."

Aiden's eyes fill with tears, and mine do the same when I realize how hurt he is.

"Aiden, no. This is all a big misunder——"

"I thought wwwe were doing okaaay. I help him as mmmuch as I can. I clean mmmy room. I do good in school. Wwwhy doesn't he wwwant mmme anymmmore?"

I grip his face in my hands, forcing him to stop and listen. "This is not because of you. This has nothing to do with anything you did or didn't do. Your uncle loves you more than anything else in this world, you hear me? He does not want to give you up. He isn't trying to take you back to your mother."

A tear rolls down his cheek. "Then wwwhy did he call her? Wwwhy does he even care about herrr?"

I sit back against the plastic racing seat and shake my head. "Sometimes, when you love people, you do stupid shit because you think it's the right thing to do. He thought he was doing the right thing, checking up on your mother and seeing if she'd want to be a part of your life. He has this idea that your life is lacking something because you don't have a mom. He thinks he isn't good enough to raise you on his own."

Aiden's eyebrows dip down. "Wwwhy wwwould he think that? He gives mmme everything I nnneed."

"Your uncle is a rare breed of human. He doubts himself, and doesn't think he's worth a damn. I think it has to do with the way his father treated him growing up. He doesn't see all the good parts inside of himself. He doesn't see how happy he makes everyone around him. He's also a stubborn idiot, but that's another story for another day."

Aiden cracks a crooked smile.

"He isn't perfect, but when he loves someone, he loves with everything he's got."

"He loves yyyou."

"I know."

"Yyyou love him too, yyyou know."

I offer Aiden a small smile. "So, whaddya say we go back home and put your uncle out of his misery? He's going crazy searching for you. We've all been."

"I'm sorry I wwworried yyyou."

I ruffle his hair and stand. "Just don't do it again. Next time you get a bright idea like this, call me, will you?"

"Deal."

"Until the end of the line, Cap'."

Aiden grins his lopsided grin that I love so much.

When we get back onto the boardwalk, I call Christopher but he doesn't answer. I shoot him a quick text letting him know that I'm with Aiden, and we're on the way to his apartment.

"Do yyyou think he'll be mmmad?" Aiden asks on our drive home.

"No. He'll want to talk about what you heard though. I think it's good for you to hear his side, and to discuss how it made you feel."

Aiden nods, glancing out the window.

My phone rings, my brother's name popping up on the screen. I pick it up on my car's Bluetooth. "Hey, Michael. Call off the search. I found Aiden. Will you let Dad and the rest of them know?"

"Mich, are you driving?"

"Yeah, I've got Aiden in the car with me."

"Can you pull over for a sec?"

"It's okay, you're on Bluetooth."

"Pull over, Michelle. I need to tell you something."

The urgency in his voice has my heart racing. I pull off the road and into a parking lot, pushing the shifter into *Park*.

"Okay, I pulled over. What's wrong?"

"Christopher is here."

"Great. Tell him to meet me at the apartment. We're on our way there now."

"No, Michelle. He's *here*. He's been in an accident."

My mouth opens but no words come out.

An accident?

No.

That's not right.

He can't be hurt.

He has to be okay.

Aiden needs him to be okay.

I need him to be okay.

Aiden leans forward in his seat. "Is he okaaay?"

"He's gonna be okay, bud. He's pretty banged up, but we're taking care of him."

"Banged up?" I echo.

"He hit a tree. The guy behind him said all he saw was Christopher's car swerve off the road and into a tree. Knocked him out on impact. Luckily, the guy stayed there to call an ambulance right away."

Swerve.

Hit a tree.

Knocked him out.

Michael's words sound garbled. I can't focus on everything he's saying. All I know is Christopher is hurt and I need to get to that hospital.

"Where are you?" Michael asks.

I lift my gaze to the windshield, and my stomach sinks down into my toes.

"I'm parked in front of *Dunkin Donuts*."

And that's when the tears start to fall.

Aiden wraps his arm around my shoulders as they shake with my sobs. "It's okay, Mmmichelle. Everything's going to be finnne."

Great. The kid is consoling me, when I should be the one consoling him.

"I'll call Dad and have him pick you guys up," Michael says. "I don't want you driving like this."

"Promise me he's okay," I choke out before Michael hangs up. "Promise he's not worse than you're letting on. Tell me the truth."

"I promise, little sis. Chris is going to be okay."

169

CHRISTOPHER

Ouch.

Hitting a tree hurts.

I don't recommend it.

Though I'd slam into it again if it meant I could hold Michelle like this a little longer.

She's asleep next to me in the hospital bed, arm draped over my stomach, head on my chest. I woke up like this, and the pain can't outweigh the surge of love I feel coursing through me.

I cracked a rib and fractured my wrist, but it could've been worse. It could've been my right arm.

Then how would I wipe my ass?

I shudder at the thought.

I look to Aiden, who's sitting in the chair next to my bed. That kid nearly killed me today, and not because of my accident. I thought I'd lost him. I thought he was on a train halfway to Timbuctoo.

Does anybody actually know where Timbuctoo is? I wouldn't know how to find him.

He has earphones in, playing a video game on Ryan's phone while Caleb plays in the chair beside him. Ryan's out on snack duty.

This many teenage boys in one room calls for sugary vending machine snacks.

Michelle's father is here too. He's talking with Michael out in the hall. Raegan stopped by earlier, but I was too out of it to talk.

It's amazing how different your life can be from one chapter to the next. If I'd gotten into a car accident back in Tennessee, my father would've been too drunk to find the hospital. My sister would've been too high. I'd be all alone.

Now, I've got people.

I've got Michelle's people.

Having her by my side opens up a whole world I've never had. And I don't want to let that go.

I don't want to let *her* go.

She stirs beside me. "If you squeeze me any tighter, I'm going to have a cracked rib too."

I smile. "Been a long time since I've heard your sleepy voice. Never thought I'd get to hear it again."

Her doe eyes peer up at me. "You almost didn't."

I lift the hand that's not connected with tubes to caress her cheek. "I'm here, Bambi. I'm okay."

She blinks through her tears. "What happened?"

I squeeze my eyes shut, knowing I have to tell the truth but wishing I didn't. "Well, I was driving around looking for Aiden. The speed limit was forty, so that's what I was doing. And all of a sudden, a kamikaze squirrel just darts out in front of me. Someone was behind me, and I didn't want to jam on my breaks. So I swerved to avoid hitting it. Then ... boom. Tree."

She stares at me with a blank expression. "A squirrel."

"Yup."

"You broke your rib and your wrist ... to avoid a squirrel."

"A *kamikaze* squirrel."

"Aren't all squirrels kamikazes?"

"Would you rather I mowed the squirrel down?"

"As opposed to this," she gestures with her hand, waving it over my body. "Yes."

"You're a monster."

She rolls her eyes, but there's a smile begging to bloom just at the corner of her mouth.

"You were right," I say, all humor gone from my tone.

She shakes her head. "Don't. Not now."

"You were right, and I should've listened to you. I should've told Aiden about his mother. Given him the choice. Instead, he caught a snippet of a really awful conversation and got the wrong idea." I slide my gaze to Aiden. "I made him think I was going to give him up."

Michelle turns my chin until my eyes return to hers. "I straightened things out. He knows you would never give him up."

I smooth my hand over her soft hair. "Where'd you end up finding him anyway?"

"At the arcade."

My eyebrows lift. "The boardwalk."

"Our place."

I tip my head down until my forehead rests against hers. "Thank you for finding him."

"I have something to tell you," she says. She holds her hand up, showing me her ring finger.

Finally.

"I broke up with Richard."

I press my lips to the back of her hand. "Are you okay?"

She nods. "I am. He wasn't the right person for me."

"No, he wasn't."

"When I was on the way here," she says, her voice low. "All I could think about was that pool ball sitting in your shoebox."

"Why the pool ball?"

"It represents us. How we started. Our relationship. Without that moment, without you and your freakish mishaps, we never would've met. Then, you left and it got stuffed into a shoebox. Hidden, but not forgotten about. Lingering in the background, just waiting for the lid to be opened up and taken out. Waiting to be remembered.

"It took me a while to remember. Part of me didn't want to. I'd buried my feelings for a reason. The pain of losing you was too much, and I've been too proud to acknowledge that the feelings I had for you never went away. It's terrifying to know that even after you broke my heart, I could still love you with every broken piece of it. I hate to admit it, but it's true. I'm scared of letting you in again. Scared of getting hurt. Scared of the what-ifs."

Her father enters the room, and a soft smile touches her lips. "But some would say it's better to give love a second chance than to never try at all."

My mouth opens, but my throat feels dry and scratchy. "Are … are you saying what I think you're saying?"

She looks up at me, and my heart falters at the sight. Love emanates from those big, beautiful brown eyes, and it's all I've dreamed of seeing.

"I love you, Christopher Hastings."

I slide my fingers through her hair and cradle her neck, tilting her face up toward mine. Every nerve ending in my body is tingling, and it's not from the painkillers. I press my lips against hers, and we let out contented sighs, succumbing to the kiss.

She fists the hospital gown and tugs me closer, tears dropping between us—hers, mine—both of us overcome by the reality of what's happening. I don't want to move, don't want to pull back for air, for fear this is all a lucid dream.

We're back.

We found our way back to each other.

Like I'd always hoped we would.

19

CHRISTOPHER

"We're a sorry pair. You with crutches, me with my cast."

Aiden chuckles. "Wwwe really arrre."

"It feels good to be home."

The doctor kept me overnight for observation, and I barely got any sleep with all the beeping and noises in the hospital.

I ease down onto the couch and pat the space beside me. "Come sit with me."

Aiden props his crutches against the armrest, and the cushion dips as he sits. "Look, Unnncle Chris—"

I lift my hand up. "Please, let me go first."

Aiden drops his eyes to his lap and nods.

"I'm sorry you had to hear part of my conversation with your mother. I'm sorry you didn't hear it from me first. I'm sorry I didn't discuss things with you beforehand. But what you heard? That wasn't me trying to give you back to her. That was me, worrying about you not having a mother figure in your life. That was me, worrying that I'm not enough. That was me, trying to do the right thing and give you a better family."

I reach over and grasp Aiden's hand in mine. "I would never,

ever give you up. No matter what. You want to know the truth? I was terrified that your mother would be clean and sober, and that she'd fight to get you back. I was even more scared that you'd want to go back to her."

Aiden shakes his head. "I don't wwwant to leave yyyou. I wwwant to stay wwwith yyyou foreverrr."

I smile and squeeze his hand. "Good, because you're stuck with me. That being said, I need you to understand that what you did was wrong. You can't disappear without telling me where you're going. You can't go off on your own. It's not safe, and not because you have Cerebral Palsy. I'd say the same thing if you were any other kid."

Aiden's wide eyes look straight into mine. "I'm sorry. I prommmise I wwwon't do that everrr again."

"And I promise to communicate with you before I do something. You deserve to know what's going on."

He nods and his shoulders visibly relax.

"Now there's one more thing I want to talk to you about." I adjust myself on the couch, turning to face him. "I want to ask your mom to surrender her rights to you. I want to become your legal guardian. If that's something you'd want, of course."

Aiden's face lights up. "Yyyes! I wwwant that."

I chuckle. "I want that too, bud. I'm not sure if she'll go for it, but I don't see why not."

"Wwwhat did she say wwwhen yyyou called her?"

I roll my lips together, pondering how I'm going to explain this one to him. We just discussed the importance of telling the truth and communicating with one another.

But sometimes, twisting the truth to spare an innocent kid's feelings is the better choice.

"She's trying to stay sober, but I don't know if she'll ever truly be clean. She knows you're in good hands."

"So she didn't wwwant mmme back," he says.

So wise beyond his years.

"No, bud. I'm sorry."

He lifts a shoulder. "It's okaaay. I don't think I'd wwwant her to wwwant mmme anyway."

I lean over and pull him into an embrace with my good arm.

"Can wwwe wwwatch Buffy?" he asks.

I grin and reach for the remote.

MICHELLE

Christopher takes the rest of the week off from work, and I'm there every day after school to take care of him.

To make out, really.

He's still injured though, so that's my excuse and I'm sticking to it.

It just feels right being with him. Somehow, we've picked up right where we left off five years ago. Madly in love, deliriously happy, and so absolutely sure that we belong together.

People say things happen for a reason.

Christopher had to leave to be there for Aiden.

I had to go my own way in order to learn the importance of forgiveness, and listening to my heart.

My inner bitch wasn't out to get me after all. I haven't heard from her since I broke up with Richard. Guess that means she's happy.

I'm happy.

It's Friday night and *Captain America: Civil War* just ended. Aiden yawns on the couch beside us, stretching his arms up over his head.

"I'm goinnng to sleep. Goodnnnight."

"Night, bud."

The second Aiden's door clicks closed, Christopher reaches for me and pulls me against him, claiming my mouth. It's not close enough, so I swing my leg over his, straddling him, careful of his broken wrist. His plump lips press to mine as I wrap my arms around his neck, threading my fingers through his thick hair.

His tongue sweeps across my bottom lip, and I let out a low moan as I open for him to deepen our kiss. His right hand inches down my lower back, stopping just above my ass. His hardness bulges through his sweatpants, giving me the perfect amount of friction. I roll my pelvis against him and his fingertips dig into my hip.

"God, I've missed kissing you," he whispers against my mouth.

"I've missed all of this."

"When my arm heals, we've got a lot of making up to do."

I grin, pressing myself against him again. "Who says we have to wait until your arm heals?"

He pulls back to look at me. "I want to do this right. I want to take you out on dates, and hold your hand. Do things proper."

"We've waited long enough. We already dated and had sex. We can skip all that beginning stuff and get right to the fun parts."

He chuckles. "The beginning stuff is the fun part. Plus I need all my extremities when I make love to you. None of this one-armed, half-assed shit."

I groan as I rock my hips against him, sucking on his bottom lip. "Are you sure you want to wait?"

His head falls back and his eyes close for a brief moment. "Yes, I'm sure. Now get off me before I change my mind."

I giggle as I trail kisses down his neck. "How long till you get your cast off again?"

"Six weeks."

I groan, dropping my forehead onto his shoulder.

"But the doctor said I should feel better before that." He tips my chin up and kisses the tip of my nose. "We have all the time in the world, Bambi. We don't have to rush. We're together now."

"I just feel like we've missed out on so much."

"Not anymore. We've got the rest of our lives to spend together. I'm not going anywhere ever again. I promise."

"No more leaving?"

"No more leaving."

"No more kamikaze squirrels?"

He grins. "No more kamikaze squirrels."

"Fine." With a huff, I slink off his lap and plop onto the couch cushion beside him.

"I actually want to run something by you. I've already talked to Aiden about it."

"Sure. What's going on?"

He sighs and adjusts his arm on the armrest. "I want to ask my sister to surrender her rights as Aiden's mother. I want to be his legal guardian."

My heart swells and my eyes widen. "Really? Do you think she'd go for it?"

"After the awful things she said to me on that phone last week?" He shrugs. "I have to try."

I reach out and squeeze his knee. "Aiden would love that."

He chews the inside of his cheek, eyebrows pinched together.

"Is there something else?" I ask.

"Are you sure you want to be with me?"

My head jerks back. "Are you serious right now?"

"I just mean, are you sure you want to take all this on? Me and Aiden, we're a package deal. It's not easy raising a teenager, let alone a teenager that isn't even your own. I want to make sure it's something you want. I want to make sure—"

My thumb gently caresses the worry lines between his brows. "I'm all in, Chris. You, Aiden. Everything. I wouldn't have it any other way."

He nods, still stuck in his own head.

"Looks like you still need some convincing." I climb back into his lap and press my lips against his. "I'll make sure there isn't a doubt in your mind that I mean everything I'm saying."

He smiles against my mouth, and we kiss until our lips are swollen into the late hours of the night.

20

CHRISTOPHER

I t's been almost a month since I spoke to my sister.

My ribs don't hurt as much as they did, and my cast will be off in another week or so.

Things with Michelle have been amazing. We've gone on dates, I've brought her flowers, she sends me dirty texts, and we sneak kisses in between classes at work.

Aiden and I have been closer than ever. I guess shit had to hit the fan in order to get where we are now.

Michelle and Aiden are sitting with me at the kitchen table while my hand holding my phone shakes.

Michelle gives us a pep-talk. "Okay, boys. Remember: Whatever happens, the outcome will not change anything between you two. You're still family, regardless of a legal piece of paper."

Aiden nods and I press the call button on the screen. "Here we go."

My sister answers almost immediately. "What?"

"Hello to you too," I grit out.

"Why are you callin' again? Didn't get the picture the last time we talked? I told you: I don't want that retar—"

"I'm calling because I want to ask you if you'd consider

signing over your rights to me" I blurt out, hoping Aiden didn't make out what she was about to say. "I want to be Aiden's legal guardian."

All three of us hold our breaths waiting for Cindy's response.

"What the hell does that mean?" she barks.

"It means you wouldn't be considered his mother, legally, anymore. I'd get to make decisions for Aiden. I'd be responsible for him, physically and financially."

I throw the financial part in there, knowing it'll help sway her decision.

"I ain't payin' you nothin'."

"You wouldn't have to pay for anything. I'd send you the paperwork, and all you have to do is sign it and mail it back to me. I'll even enclose a stamped return envelope for you."

"If it'll get you to stop harrassin' me about this damn kid, then fine."

My heart pounds faster. "You'll do it?"

"I said yes, didn't I?"

"Cindy, thank you so—"

The call ends.

"She said yyyes?" Aiden asks.

I nod, mouth hanging open in shock at how easy that was. "Yeah, bud. She said yes."

Michelle flings her arms around Aiden, squeezing him until he laughs. "You're ours, now!"

He chuckles and looks up at me. "I always wwwas."

* * *

"What you want to do is line up your shot. Keep your left arm still, and only move your right one when you push the stick forward."

"Push the stick forward," I echo, nodding like a zombie.

Michelle jerks upright, hand flying to her hip. "Are you listening to anything I'm saying, or are you just staring at my ass while I'm bent over?"

I wrap my arms around her waist, dipping my head down to meet her lips. "I'm definitely staring."

She pretends to be angry, but her smile breaks through. "Good."

I took Michelle out for dinner, and now she's teaching me how to play pool.

Or at least we're pretending to care about playing pool, when all we want to do is rush home to my drawer full of condoms. Aiden's sleeping over Jordan's house tonight, which means Michelle and I have the apartment all to ourselves.

Michelle lifts up onto her toes and places a slow, sensual kiss on my lips that I feel all the way in my toes. "You're the one who wanted to play pool."

"That was before my nephew packed his bag and went to his best friend's house."

I drag my nose along her neck and bite the sensitive skin just below her ear. A soft whisper of a moan escapes her as her fingers dig into my back.

We've been torturing each other all night. Teasing kisses, sexy nibbles, and fingers brushing against sensitive spots. We're both about to combust from the pent-up sexual tension, added on top of the past five years.

There's no way we're finishing this pool game.

I grab Michelle's hand and yank her toward the exit. She squeals and her pool cue clatters to the floor.

With one hand on the steering wheel, and the other squeezing her thigh for dear life, Michelle kisses and licks my neck, my jaw, my ear the whole way home.

Home.

I never really looked at my crappy apartment as a home. Not until Michelle started spending time there with us. She completes me and Aiden in a way that I never expected.

Once we're inside my apartment, we fumble around in the darkness, trying to undress with our lips fused together. We're kicking out of our shoes, tearing our shirts over our heads, flinging our pants wherever they land.

By the time I flick the lights on in my bedroom, we're down to our last few scraps of clothes. I pause, eyes ablaze as they roam over Michelle's bare body. Her chest heaves, breasts begging to be freed from the red cotton bra she's wearing. The color pops against her fair skin and dark hair, drawing all your attention. I'm frozen where I stand as she reaches back and unhooks the clasp. The straps fall off her shoulders, slowly sliding down her arms as she lets it drop to the floor. I want to swirl my tongue around her pert pink nipples, take each one into my mouth and give them the attention they deserve.

But not yet.

I want to appreciate this moment. Savor every second, not taking any of it for granted because I know what it's like to be without her.

My heart races as her fingers hook inside her red boy shorts, peeling them down her legs and baring herself to me.

"God damn," I rasp.

She's *mine*. Heart, body, and soul.

And I'm hers. I always have been.

Her cheeks turn a rosy pink color and she edges toward me. "Your turn."

I tug on the elastic on my boxer-briefs and my dick springs forward, reaching for her, while my skin heats under her hungry gaze.

She takes another step closer, reaching out to run her fingertips along the ridges in my abdomen.

"I forgot how good you look," she whispers.

I let my hands roam around her curves. One caresses her breast, her body shivering when I run my thumb over her nipple. The other hand slides around to cup the swell of her perfect ass. I pull her body against mine, and she meets my mouth halfway, moaning as my tongue sweeps inside in search of hers.

Succumbing to the agony of taking things slow, our kisses soon become frantic. I feel her hand wrap around my dick just as my fingers slide along her clit, and we both sigh as we finally give in.

My hand disappears further between her legs, skimming my fingers along her wetness. She tilts her hips as a plea to keep going, and I give her what she wants. I spin her around so her back hits the wall, and drop to my knees. My middle finger slips inside her, while my tongue draws languid circles around her clit.

Michelle fists handfuls of my hair, her breathy moans filling the room. I grasp behind her knee and pull her leg over my shoulder before dipping another finger inside. She's tight and hot and wet, and tastes like heaven. I work her until she's panting, begging for release.

"Oh God, Chris," she whimpers, arching into my touch.

"Yes, baby. Come for me."

Michelle cries out my name, her pussy clenching around my fingers as waves of pleasure rack through her body. I lap up every last drop until her arms and legs go limp. When I stand, I glide my dick up and down her seam, coating myself in her arousal.

From under heavy lids, she looks up at me. "Fuck me, Christopher. You can make love to me later, but please, I need you to fuck me first."

With a growl, I lift her up into my arms and stalk to my bed. She bounces onto the mattress when I drop her down, and she props herself up on her elbows while I grab a condom from my nightstand. My dick aches as I roll the thin rubber onto my length, and I'm afraid I won't last long once she takes me inside.

I climb on top of her, caging her in with my arms while she spreads her thighs to wrap them around me. I dip down, kissing her stomach, up her ribs, and stopping to take each pebbled nipple into my mouth, licking and sucking on them until I've had my fill.

I look into those big brown eyes of hers as I press my tip to her entrance. She arches her back, willing me to continue further. I grin as I lower my lips to hers and kiss her senseless. Then I plunge inside, holding myself there, relishing the feeling of being this connected to her once again.

I drop my forehead to hers, looking down between us to watch as I drag myself out of her, only to dive back in. I groan into her mouth as my tongue swirls around hers, and she digs her heels into my ass, spurring me to thrust harder, deeper.

Nothing compares to this moment, knowing I have her, realizing that we're back in each other's arms after all the pain and heartache we endured.

Michelle cries out each time I slam into her, meeting me thrust for thrust, the sound of our bodies smacking together in a maddening rhythm. She lifts her arms above her head and plants her hands against the wall. I slip my hand between our bodies and play with her clit until she comes. I lose any semblance of control when I feel her orgasm, the way she tightens around my dick, the way her body writhes underneath me.

And I let go.

I surrender everything to her, everything I've got, every part of me.

It always belonged to her.

"I love you, Christopher," she whispers, over and over again, as I pump my release.

My body stills, muscles rigid, toes curled, in the most explosive orgasm of my life.

And then a loud crack echoes through the room, one corner of my mattress jerking downward.

Michelle's eyes go wide as she grips onto my shoulders. "Did we just break your bed?"

"Pretty sure we did."

Her giggle turns into a full-blown laugh and soon she's hysterical. I can't contain my grin. Watching her laugh, witnessing her happiness, it's like seeing snow for the first time.

Pure magic.

She sobers when she notices my expression, touching her fingers to my cheek. "Are you okay? What's wrong? I can buy you another bed if you don't have the money."

I shake my head, choking back the emotion lodged in my throat. "I can't believe this is real. You're here. We're really together."

Her eyes glisten and a small smile touches her lips. "And we always will be."

EPILOGUE

5 YEARS LATER

Michelle

"Is it timmme yyyet?"

I lean over and check the timer on my phone. "Two more minutes."

"This is takinnng foreverrr," Aiden says.

"It's only been thirty seconds." I smile and drag my gaze over to Christopher. "You're going to burn a hole through our floor if you keep pacing like that."

He huffs a breath and plants his hands on his hips. "What if it's a girl? I won't know what to do with a girl. I only know how to raise a boy. And even then, I don't know what to do with a *baby* boy. You have to know how to change their diapers, and how much milk to put in their bottles, and why they're crying." He stops and turns to me, eyes wide. "They can't talk. How does anybody know why they're crying?"

Aiden shakes his head with a smirk dancing on his lips. "Yyy-ou'll figure it out."

I glance at the timer again and pat the space next to me on the tile floor. "Come sit with me."

188

Christopher slides his back down the bathroom wall, clasping my hand in his.

"Aiden's right," I say, resting my head on his shoulder. "We're going to figure everything out together. I don't know any more about babies than you do. But we can ask our doctor. We can also call Raegan any time we have questions. She's the baby expert now."

Christopher's eyes double in size. "What if we have twins, like Rae and Jaxon?"

I shrug. "Then you're on your own because I can't handle twins."

Aiden chuckles.

I'm trying to lighten the mood for Christopher's sake, but I'm nervous too. We've only been married for a year, and I was hoping to get a little more time together before adding a baby into the mix.

But if there's one thing I've learned, it's that everything happens for a reason. So I have to trust that the universe is sending us a baby now because this is how our story is destined to go.

And I know I'm pregnant. I don't need to wait for this pregnancy test to reveal two pink lines for me to know. I can feel it. My inner bitch is never wrong.

Buzz.

The boys simultaneously jump up, lurching for the cup on the counter. Christopher trips over his own two feet and ends up sprawled out in the middle of the bathroom floor.

Aiden stares down at the stick.

"Well?" I ask.

"Wwwe're having a baby!"

A smile spreads across my face as I stand. "That baby is going to have the best big cousin ever."

Aiden wraps me in a hug and I bury my face in his chest. The lanky little kid shot up over the past few years and is now taller than me. He's been working extra hard at physical therapy, and bulked up the muscles in his arms and chest a bit. He even gets his hair cut now.

It's because of a girl he's trying to impress, but still.

My boy is all grown up.

He's going to be dorming at college in New York starting in the fall. (Which Christopher is *also* freaking out about.) I'm sad that he's leaving us, especially now with a baby on the way. But I won't hold him back.

That kid is born to fly.

"What are we going to do with your uncle?" I whisper.

We turn to look down at Christopher, who's kneeling on the floor, covering his face with his hands.

"He'll be finnne," Aiden says. "He's goinnng to be the best dad everrr."

That's when the tears sting my eyes, realization setting in.

Imagining my husband holding our newborn child in his arms, wondering if he or she will have his gorgeous hazel eyes, watching his face light up when the baby does something cute.

Our child gets to grow up with the most loving, selfless, incredible human being I've ever known as his or her father. And I couldn't be luckier.

I crouch down on the floor beside Christopher, stroking his hair. "We're having a baby."

He flicks his watery gaze to mine, tears rolling down his cheeks. "I'm so happy, Bambi."

"Me too."

We have something not every couple does: We've experienced what it's like to be without each other. It allows us to appreciate every moment we have that much more. We know how precious our time together is. How we wouldn't be where we are today if we weren't truly meant to be.

Christopher wipes his eyes with the backs of his hands, and gestures for Aiden to sit down with us. "You know this doesn't change anything, right bud?"

"It's a baby," Aiden says. "It's goinnng to change everrrything."

Christopher rests his hand on Aiden's shoulder. "You know what I mean. I don't want you to think for one second that you're anything less than my son just because we're having a baby."

Aiden nods. "I have to tell yyyou guys sommmething I've been thinnnking about for a wwwhile."

My stomach tightens. "What's going on?"

"I don't wwwant to dorm wwwhen I go to college."

"What?" My voice echoes against the tile. "You've been so excited about it. Why the sudden change?"

"I always knnnew yyyou guys wwwould have a baby one day. And I nnnever had any siblings. I wwwant to be around wwwhen the baby comes. I don't wwwant to mmmiss anything."

Christopher and I exchange glances. I don't want Aiden to miss out on a fun college experience. Especially not if he's only staying home because he's afraid of being replaced by this new baby.

On the other hand, I don't want to push him to do something he's not comfortable with.

It's hard being a parent. You never know if you're doing the right thing.

"Is there another reason you don't want to dorm there?" Christopher asks, reading my mind. "Traveling back and forth from the city every day might be exhausting."

"Nnno. If yyyou guys wwwweren't having a baby, I wwwouldn't stay home. Nnno offense."

I throw my head back and laugh. "God, I love your honesty, kid."

Aiden grins. "I just wwwant to be here for the baby."

"You might rethink that once you hear the late-night scream fests Raegan keeps talking about."

Christopher's head falls back against the wall with a thud. "Can I dorm at college instead?"

I smack his arm playfully. "Hey, you put this baby in me. You're going to deal with it when it comes out."

Aiden covers his ears, cringing. "Didn't nnneed to hear that."

Christopher chuckles and claps him on the back. They stand, and extend their hands to pull me up.

"Let's get this mama some ice cream and a foot rub!" Christopher swoops me up in his arms.

"Oh, God. Just don't drop me," I say, clutching onto his neck.

"Never."

He carries me into the hallway, past the memories we've made through the years hanging on the wall. We bought a house together two years ago, and the first thing we did was decorate it with pictures.

"Let's hope the baby doesn't innnherit yyyour clumsiness," Aiden calls behind us.

I bury my face in Christopher's shirt, shoulders shaking with laughter.

"For the record, this baby is going to be on *my* team." Christopher lowers me onto the couch, waving his index finger between us. "You two want to be Cap' and Bucky? Well, the baby is going to be the Robin to my Batman."

I tap my finger against my chin, closing one eye. "Captain America could destroy Batman. You know that, right?"

"Not the point."

"Okay, Batman" I say, tugging on his shirt until he brings his mouth down to mine. "But you have to get the black leather costume to go along with it."

He grins and plants a chaste kiss on my lips. "You've got yourself a deal. I could definitely get into some roleplay."

While Aiden's scooping ice cream into three large bowls, I nudge Christopher and lower my voice. "Do you really think it's a good idea for Aiden to stay here instead of dorming?"

He shrugs. "I'm not sure. We can't exactly force him to go, and it *is* a hell of a lot cheaper if he lives here."

"I know. I just want him to have the perfect freshman experience. I don't want him to regret it."

"We'll give him a semester to see how he feels. Maybe he'll change his mind."

Aiden brings me three heaping scoops of mint chocolate chip before carrying in the other two bowls. He relaxes back onto the couch and we spend the remainder of the night watching movies, curled up together with blankets and pillows.

Captain and Bucky, and now a Robin for my Batman.

The End

* * *

Want to find out what's really going on between Raegan and Principal Waters? Keep reading for the prologue and first chapter of *Hating the Boss*, an Amazon Top 30 Bestseller!

HATING THE BOSS

Days Left Until Summer Break: 80
Jaxon

"Yes, Jaxon. Oh, God. Yes!"

See that woman? The one having the best orgasm of her life? That's my girl, Raegan. She's beautiful. Long, blond hair. Striking green eyes. Thick thighs. More-than-a-handful tits. She's perfect. This moment is perfect.

It's been a long time coming. Things weren't always this great. We had a bit of a rough start. I accused her of stealing my dead grandmother's ring. She swore she didn't. We waged war against each other for months.

But all that's behind us now.

"I love you, Raegan," I whisper in her ear. "I love you so much."

She cups my face, gazing into my eyes. "I love you too."

It's my turn to pump my release and when I'm done, I hold her in my arms. We're sated and relaxed. Happy. For the first time in a long time, everything feels right.

Raegan's stomach lets out a loud growl. I chuckle. "I'll get our tacos." I plant a kiss on her forehead and roll out of bed.

Life is crazy. A chance encounter can tilt your entire world on its axis. You can't always see the reason why things happen in the beginning, but eventually, it all clicks into place. Everything makes sense.

One second you're miserable, and the next you're making post-sex tacos for your girlfriend on Valentine's Day with a goofy smile plastered on your face.

I carry our plates into my bedroom, water bottles tucked under each of my elbows.

Raegan's out of bed, hunched over my open dresser drawer.

What's she looking for?

My body stills when I glance down at the blue velvet box she's clutching in her hand.

No. It can't be. "What are you doing?"

Tears well in her wide eyes. "Jax, I can explain."

The plates slam as I drop them on top of the dresser. I yank the box from her fingers and flip open the top, staring at the sparkling ring in disbelief.

See that guy? The one whose life just crumbled before his eyes? That's me, Jaxon.

Biggest chump in the fucking world.

SIX MONTHS EARLIER

RAEGAN

Days Left Until School Starts: 30

Did you know there's an entire playlist on Spotify called *Badass Slow-Motion Walking Songs?*

Imagine that scene in a movie when a car or building explodes. Now picture the actor walking away from it in slow motion, flames roaring around him, smoke billowing into the atmosphere. He's totally unfazed by the fact that he could be hit by flying debris at any moment. Notice the song playing in the background? It's a rock song, lots of drums, and it amplifies the man's badassness as he leaves the fiery scene.

That's how I envisioned myself leaving the courthouse on the day my divorce was finalized.

I had the playlist ready to go on my phone and everything. Earbuds? *Nope.* I was going to blast that shit the whole way across the parking lot.

But when the sun hits my face as I exit the courthouse, all I want to do is cry. And take a nap. Then cry some more.

Seven years I'd been married. Might not seem long to people who've been together for decades, but it felt like an eternity for me. I tried to make it work. I gave and I compromised. I cooked, I cleaned. I gave him a blowjob every night. *Every night.* Don't tell me I wasn't dedicated.

It didn't matter though. No matter what I did, it wasn't good enough. Didn't change the fact that I was married to an asshole. In Andrew's defense, he didn't mean to be an asshole. His father's a controlling prick, so he didn't know any different.

In the beginning, Andrew was sweet. Doting. At least, I thought he was. I was young. Turns out you don't know much about love or what you stand for when you're twenty. That's why they tell you not to get a tattoo until you're at least twenty-five. They say your brain isn't fully equipped to make long-term decisions before then. And when I say *they*, I mean the proverbial "they." You can hate them all you want, but *they* are always right.

It took me a while to realize that what I once thought was caring was actually possessive. What I thought was confidence was just condescending. Don't get me wrong, Andrew wasn't the worst person I could've been with. He didn't beat me or anything.

My mom says that's how you know something's wrong: You start downplaying your unhappiness and comparing it to domestic abuse.

Sometimes, I'd wished he would hit me. Just once. At least then I wouldn't have felt so guilty about leaving him.

That's sick. I realize that now.

Needless to say, I wanted this divorce. I'd been the one who'd asked for it. I'd reached my breaking point. Now I know why people call it that. You bend so much that you eventually break in half. Two parts: Who you once were, and the angry, resentful person you've become.

In the end, I gave him the house, the dog, my full bookcase, and all my Christmas decorations. Even my favorite sugarplum fairy ornament I'd had since I was a kid. I packed up the essentials and left everything else behind. That's how badly I wanted out. That, and the fact that I couldn't afford to fight him for any of it in court.

So how come I'm not slow-mo walking to my car right now? I should be thrilled and relieved that this is over.

I swing myself into my car, turn the key in the ignition, and crank up the air conditioning. As the stream of air cools my skin, I take a minute to scroll through my missed calls and texts.

Becca: Congrats! You're a free woman now!
    Mary: Congratulations! It's all over now
    Sammi: Woohoo! Moving on to brighter skies.
    Andrea: Yasss queen! Single & ready to mingle
    Kerry: Ding, dong, the dick is gone!

It's weird that everyone's congratulating me. It's even weirder when I think back to these same friends congratulating me on my wedding day.

Should I feel proud of being a divorcee? I feel as if I'm wearing a scarlet D on my chest. Like I should run and hide before people with pitchforks try to tar and feather me in the middle of town square.

I don't think my small town in New Jersey has a town square, but still. It could happen.

I click on Becca's name and lift the phone to my ear.

"Hey! How'd everything go?"

I sigh. "It went fine. I'm just exhausted."

"I'm sure. Why don't you go home and take a nap? Then you'll be recharged for tonight."

"I don't think I'm feeling up to coming out tonight."

"Oh, no. You are not getting out of this one. You can't sit home and mope around. You need to be with your friends. Your very excited friends who got babysitters to watch their asshole children for the night."

I slump forward and rest my forehead against the steering wheel. "I don't feel like celebrating."

"Then you can sit at the bar and cry into your mojito. You're coming out."

"Fine. But it's your fault if the townspeople stone me to death."

"What? Is this another one of your book references that I don't get?"

"Never mind. I'll see you tonight."

Chucking my phone onto the seat beside my purse, I glance out the windshield just in time to catch my now ex-husband waltzing out of the courthouse.

In the year it took us to get divorced, Andrew lost a good ten pounds. I'd always tried to convince him to come running with me when we were married. *I only run if I'm being chased* was his response. Funny how he suddenly found the desire to get in shape once I was out of the picture. Bastard looks better than he did when we first met.

I, on the other hand, found the ten pounds he'd lost, and tacked on another five for good measure. I'd lost my drive and stopped working out. I envy the people who stop eating when they're stressed. I'm an emotional eater. I eat my feelings, and unfortunately, they aren't fat free. They taste a lot like Ben and Jerry's.

I peel my eyes away from the man I used to love and back out of my parking spot. Instead of leaving the courthouse to my Spotify playlist like a badass, I'm crying to Don Henley's *Sometimes Love Just Ain't Enough*.

* * *

"I am *not* going in there."

Becca tugs on my elbow. "Come on. She already spotted us."

My bottom lip juts out. "But there's balloons."

"I swear I told her not to get them. You know Kerry."

The bouncer hands my license back and jerks his thumb toward the embarrassing scene that awaits me. "Those balloons are funny."

I glare at him. "Good. You can have 'em."

"They're trying to be supportive and cheer you up," Becca says. "We just want you to be happy again."

"I know, I know." I blow out a puff of air and lift my chin. "All right. Let's get this over with."

We step inside the bar and I plaster a smile on my face. One thing my marriage taught me is how to hide my emotions from anyone and everyone. I've become so good at lying, even to myself, I could probably pass a lie detector test. I'd be a valuable asset if the CIA ever wanted me.

My friends wave excitedly, dressed to the nines with hair and makeup on point. We are the epitome of women in their thirties. It's like we're stuck in limbo: Too old to let loose the way we did in our twenties, but too young to feel content at home with a pair of knitting needles.

I cringe as I gaze up at the six shimmery gold balloons, each of them broadcasting my humiliating news to the entire bar: *I'm not with stupid anymore. Divorced AF. Ditched the dick. Unhitched. Just divorced. Legally single.*

To make matters worse, Kerry's holding a black sash. I don't know what it says yet, but I wonder if it'd be strong enough to act as a noose.

"Congrats, mama!" Kerry raises the sash above my head.

I duck out of the way. "I love you, Kerr, but I'm not putting that thing on. The balloons are more than enough."

Her cheerful expression falls. "Here." She shoves a mixed drink into my hand. "Maybe you'll change your mind after a few of these."

Mary, Andrea, and Sammi offer me smiles laced with pity.

"Oh, no," I say, waving my free hand. "Don't look at me like that. It's done and over with. Let's just forget about it."

"How did it go today?" Andrea asks.

"Quick and easy. If you ladies ever need to get divorced, the Divorce Center is the way to go."

"Good to know," Kerry says. "I'll make that the new threat I throw at Brad the next time he decides to stay out late after work."

"He's still doing that?"

"Don't wanna talk about it." Kerry raises her glass. "To Rae. Let's get you laid tonight."

I shake my head but drink to her toast anyway.

"What?" she asks. "The best way to get over someone ..."

"She just got divorced," Sammi says. "Give her some time."

"I need to lose this weight first." I gesture to my stomach. I'm wearing a flowy top, but we've all seen the bulge underneath that's currently hanging over the waistband of my jeans.

"Oh, thank God," Kerry says, wiping her forehead for effect. "I was hoping you weren't accepting this as your new physique."

Mary and Becca swat each of Kerry's arms and exclaim her name in unison.

"It's okay," I say. "We don't have to pretend like I haven't gained some weight."

"You should come kick-boxing with me," Andrea says.

"I will definitely take you up on that. We've got one month until work starts in September, and I plan on walking through the doors of Roosevelt Elementary a changed woman."

"Good for you," Becca says.

Andrea's glass slams onto the bar. "Speaking of work, did you read the board minutes?" She pulls her phone from her cleavage and scrolls through it at lightning speed. "Dr. Reynolds was let go!"

My eyes go wide. *Our principal was fired?*

"Are you serious?" Mary snatches Andrea's phone and we huddle around it to read the e-mail.

Board minutes are like gossip columns in the education world. Salaries, firings, and retire-ings are e-mailed to every employee working for the Board of Ed.

"Good riddance. I've had enough of these female principals on a power trip," Kerry says. "We need some testosterone in our school. Someone to scare all those little shits into behaving."

Sammi shakes her head. "It's going to take a lot more than a man in a suit to scare our students."

"Forget the kids," Mary says. "We need to teach parents how to discipline their children. I'm tired of getting hit, and then asked what I did to make the kid hit me."

"Amen to that."

The six of us have been friends for as long as we've been teaching at Roosevelt Elementary school. We refer to ourselves as the kindergarten dream team. Not every grade level in our building is as tight-knit as we are. Not every teacher pulls her own weight. But in our group, we're like a well-oiled machine.

You need a good support system when you're battling a room full of five-year olds. Teaching kindergarten isn't for the faint of heart.

I shudder at the thought of going back to work with my maiden name. The looks, the whispers, the questions, all from co-workers who act like they care just because they want the gossip. At least I have thirty-one more days of summer bliss.

I lean toward the bartender who's mixing a drink in front of us. "Can we have a round of shots, please?"

"What's your poison?" he asks.

"Whatever's strong enough to help me forget about these balloons hovering over my head."

He chuckles. "Got it."

Soon after we down our shots, the bartender pours us another round. "These are from those gentlemen over there."

All six of our heads swivel in the direction of the bartender's finger. Four smiling men raise their own shot glasses.

"What does this mean?" Sammi asks. "What do we do?"

Andrea pats her on the back and hands her a glass. "We do the shot, babe."

"Won't they think we'll want to sleep with them if we do the shot?"

"They're men. They already think everyone wants to sleep with them." Kerry lifts her chin and throws back the amber liquid.

I wrap my arm around Sammi's tense shoulders. "The bartender poured them right in front of us. No one's getting roofied. Now smile at the nice men and drink your free alcohol."

"They're coming over here." Kerry nudges me toward the front of our circle. "You're single now. Go get 'em, tiger."

I shoot daggers at her over my shoulder. On second thought, maybe that sash will come in handy. I could use it to strangle *her* instead of myself.

"Do that thing," Mary whispers, and the girls nod.

I scan the men as they approach. "The short one is the leader. He's the most muscular because he's overcompensating for his height. I say he's in finance. The tall, scrawny one looks like he's a doctor. He's the quiet type. The blond knows he's good-looking, but he's not a douche about it. I say he's a personal trainer."

My eyes land on the fourth man, lingering much longer than they did on his three friends. Tall, dark, and handsome doesn't quite do him justice. Thick, tousled hair. A clean-shaven, prominent jawline. Broad shoulders. He's the only one in the group wearing a suit—a suit that looks like it's tailored perfectly to his body. You know when you can just tell a guy is fit underneath his clothes? The way his shirt stretches across his chest, the tapering at the waist. Yeah, that's him.

Also unlike his friends, who are surveying each of us to figure out which one they want to hit on, this one's eyes are zeroed in on me. He walks with a confident stride, lips curved into a flirty smirk. It's the look of a man who knows what he wants. And he expects to get it.

"What about him?" Andrea asks.

"He looks like an executive of some sort. Definitely in a position of power. And judging by the fit of those pants, I'd put money on him having a fantastic ass."

The girls burst into giggles just as the men arrive.

"What are you ladies laughing about?" the short one asks. The leader always speaks first. *Point for me.*

"Oh, nothing," I say. "Inside joke."

Mr. Sexy in a Suit shoves his hands into his pockets. "How much money would you put down?"

My nose scrunches. "What?"

"You said you'd bet that I have a fantastic ass. How much would you wager on that?"

I clench my jaw to keep it from falling open. "What do you read lips?"

"I do," he says with a cocky grin.

I tap my finger against my chin as I make a show of assessing his body once more. "I'd bet fifty bucks I'm right."

"That's a confident bet."

"I'm a confident woman." *At least I was before seven years of marriage stifled me.*

Mary rests her elbow on my shoulder. "Fifty bucks from each of you says my girl is right about everything else she said about you too."

The men exchange glances before their pint-sized leader speaks for them. "You're on. Let's hear it."

I point to each of them. "Doctor. Finance. Personal trainer."

Their eyebrows lift as they dip into their wallets and place their cash in my hand.

Mr. Sexy in a Suit narrows his dark eyes. "And I'm just the guy with the nice ass?"

"That hasn't been proven yet," I remind him. "But I'd say you run things at your job. The boss, like a CEO or something."

A smirk tugs at his lips. "How'd you do that?"

"It's a gift. A weird gift that serves no purpose or utilizes any real talent."

"I wouldn't say that. That was pretty impressive. Do you work for the FBI?"

I lean closer to him and say, "If I told you, I'd have to kill you."

He laughs, revealing a set of perfect pearly whites. It's a stark contrast from his tan skin. I'd also like to note that his laugh is sexy. You don't realize how important a person's laugh is until you're on a date with someone whose laugh sounds like a dying mongoose.

I hold my hand out, palm facing up. "So are you going to ante up?"

"I don't have cash on me, but I'd love to buy you and your friends another round."

I pretend to mull it over. "Hmm. Not sure that'll cover your debt."

He dips down, closing the gap between us to position his lips at my ear. "I can come up with other ways to repay you."

Heat crawls up my neck and into my cheeks. This guy is used to getting his way. I'd bet girls throw themselves at him on the regular. I try to appear unaffected and hike a shoulder. "I'll take another shot of whiskey to start."

I peer up at him as the bartender takes his order. Everything about him is smooth. His skin, his voice. *Those lips.*

It's been so long since I've been kissed. I mean *really* kissed. A hands-in-the-hair, bodies wrapped around each other, all-consuming kiss.

Somewhere along the line, the desire I'd had for Andrew turned into disgust. Resentment will do that to you. It trickles into your blood like a poison, slow at first, until it's coursing through your veins. It overrides every other feeling you have, making it impossible to see through the blurriness of anger and disappointment.

I snap back to the present moment when a shot glass is handed to me. The stranger clinks his beer bottle against it and takes a long swig. His eyes flick up at the balloons. "Those for you?"

I grimace at the reminder. "Yup."

"Sorry to hear that."

"Everyone else seems to think congratulations are in order."

He shakes his head. "Divorces are sad."

"You wouldn't think so with how many couples were in the courtroom today."

"Just because it's common doesn't make it any less tragic."

He's right. His honesty puts me at ease with this conversation. Either that or the whiskey is melting my reserve.

"I feel like a failure," I confess. "Just another idiot who married the wrong person."

"You're not an idiot. Everyone makes mistakes. At least you had good enough sense to correct it. Do you know how many people stay stuck in their mistakes?"

I tilt my head to the side, turning his words over in my mind. "That actually makes me feel a little better."

"Just a little? Guess I'll have to keep trying."

My eyes bounce back and forth between his eyes, smiles tugging at both of our mouths. Flirting like this breathes some much-needed life into my lungs. *I've missed this.*

Andrea pokes her head between us. "Are you single?"

The sexy suit keeps his eyes fixed on me when he says, "I am. Wouldn't've come over here if I wasn't."

She fans herself with her glittery clutch. "Sexy and a gentleman? He's just the guy you need tonight, Rae." She winks and bounces back to our friends.

I'm about to apologize for my friend's forwardness when I realize something. Why should I apologize? Andrea is being herself. Nothing wrong with that. I'm sure this cocky man in a suit wouldn't think twice about apologizing for anything he says.

I've apologized to Andrew enough to last me a lifetime—mostly for things I didn't need to apologize for in the first place.

"So what's Rae short for?" the Sexy Suit asks.

"Raegan." I extend my hand toward him. "And you are?"

"Jaxon."

When his large hand engulfs mine, goosebumps spread up my arm. He doesn't let go right away, his coffee-colored eyes penetrating mine.

Black coffee. No cream or sugar. Just the rich, bold taste. *Wouldn't I love a sip.*

It feels like forever since I've touched a holding hand that felt like this. It feels like forever since I've touched a holding hand *period*. I didn't realize how starved I've been for affection until now.

I wonder how his hands would feel on my body …

I pull away before I start humping his leg like a dog. "So, are you really a CEO?"

"Something like that. I actually got a promotion today. Hence the suit."

"Congratulations. What do you—"

"Are we gonna dance or what?" Kerry interrupts.

I smile up at Jaxon. "My friends are heathens, as you can see."

He laughs. "Dance with your friends. I'm not going anywhere."

I arch an eyebrow. *Why?* I want to ask. Why waste your time on me when you can have any girl in this place eating out of the palm of your hand?

Kerry yanks me away from him before I can say anything, and I'm pulled into the middle of the dance floor.

"That man is *fine*," Andrea shouts over the music.

Sammi nods eagerly. "He looks really into you."

Becca nudges me with her elbow. "Did you get his number?"

"The only thing I got was whiplash. Why did you pull me over here like that? We were in the middle of a conversation."

Kerry rolls her eyes. "You need to play hard to get. Make him work for it."

"Work for what?"

"You know what."

I shake my head. "I can't go home with him."

"Why not?" Mary asks. "No harm in it if you're careful."

"You wasted your twenties with ass face," Andrea says. "You're getting a second chance now. Have fun. Let loose."

"Have sex." Kerry wiggles her eyebrows.

Sex with a stranger? Can I do that? I've only had sex while in monogamous relationships. Would I be able to bare my body to someone I don't know for one night?

I look to Sammi for backup, but she shrugs. "If you're going to have sex with a random, do it with that guy."

I scoff. "So much for being the goody-two-shoes of our group."

"What? He's gorgeous."

I laugh. *That he is.* "Let's just dance and enjoy your kid-free night out."

"Say it louder for the mamas in the back!" Andrea raises her arms overhead and gyrates her hips.

We giggle and dance the night away in our impenetrable circle. I lose track of how many shots we down. It feels *so* good to enjoy myself without having to check the time. Andrew would get angry whenever I went out with the girls. Once nine o'clock hit, he'd send text after text, demanding I come home.

So I did.

Disgust racks through my body. *God,* when did I become this passive, meek woman? No wonder I gained weight. I stopped taking care of myself, too busy catering to Andrew's wants and needs.

What about *my* needs?

Why did I allow them to take a back seat?

Why did I let someone else dictate how my life should go?

An explosion goes off within me.

It's an awakening.

Or maybe it's just the alcohol.

Whatever it is, I know one thing for certain: Never again will I be the person I was in that marriage.

From this moment on, I'm going to do the things *I* want to do. Say the things *I* want to say. And I'm going to take the things *I* want to have.

No apologies.

No backing down.

I'm going to live the life *I* want.

I glance at Jaxon, who's watching me from his stool at the bar.

It's going to start tonight.

Everything's about to change.

JAXON

"She's seriously hot. Did you call dibs yet? Because if not, dibs."

I shoot Dan a glare that reads *hands off, motherfucker.*

His hands raise on either side of his blond head. "Roger that."

Shaun jerks his thumb toward the balloons. "Divorced chicks are awesome in bed. They've got all that pent-up frustration from being unhappy with their husbands for so long."

Smith shakes his head. "It's disturbing that you know this."

"What can I say? I have a type."

Dan chuckles. "Is that how you found Carrie on Match? Short male with small dick looking for sexually frustrated divorcee."

"Fuck you." Shaun tips his beer back and then sets the empty bottle onto the bar. "I'm going to take a piss."

I turn to Dan. "You know he's touchy about his height."

Dan waves me off. "Pfft. He's fine. His ego is big enough to withstand it."

My eyes drift over to Raegan. Again. They've been drawn to her since the second she walked into the bar. Gorgeous face. Long blond hair. Tight jeans. Full tits spilling out of her top. She has everything it takes to catch a man's attention. But that's not hard to do. Wave any scrap of food in front of a dog, he'll start to salivate.

The real feat is *keeping* a man's attention. And Raegan's keeping mine for three reasons.

Reason One: She read me and my friends like a book. She's perceptive, which tells me she's smart. Intelligence is sexy to a man.

Notice how I said *to a man*. If a guy's intimidated by a woman's brain, it means he's insecure about his own intelligence. Also, he probably has a small pecker.

Reason Two: Raegan was embarrassed by the balloons her friends brought her. She doesn't want her personal business to be put on display, which shows she isn't an attention-seeker. I'm not into narcissists. Been there, done that.

Reason Three: She's confident. This is where people tend to get confused. Some women claim to be confident when in reality, they're just plain rude. There's a difference between confident and conceited.

Raegan looked me in the eye and smiled, but didn't act like she was better than anyone. She wasn't trying to be sexy or funny. Plus, there was something honest in her eyes. Vulnerable. Maybe the hurt in me sensed the hurt within her.

Needless to say, I'm intrigued.

"Are you going to dance with her, or are you going to stare at her like some creeper?" Dan asks.

"I'm giving her space. She's with her friends."

"Don't wait too long. You don't want someone else taking her home at the end of the night."

I arch an eyebrow. "She might not want to be taken home by anyone at the end of the night."

"She will if you play your cards right."

"I don't need to play games to get a girl."

"Well, you need to do something," he says. "I know your hand is tired of jerking off in the shower every night."

"First of all," Shaun says, back from the bathroom, "how do you know he jerks off in the shower every night?"

"Jealous?"

Shaun laughs. "Hardly. But he has a point, Jax. It's been long enough. Don't you think it's time you broke your dry spell?"

I drain the rest of my beer. "I think you guys worry too much about my dick."

"Or you're not worried enough." Shaun claps me on the back. "I hate that bitch for doing such a number on you, man."

My stomach clenches at the reminder. "Change the subject."

"All right, all right. I'm just saying——"

"You've said plenty. Your turn to get the next round." Smith nudges Shaun toward the bar.

I give Smith an appreciative nod.

"You know he's just worried about you," Smith says. "We all are."

"Look, I wanted to come out tonight to celebrate, not to talk about my past. My life is finally back on track. I don't need to be reminded of my failures."

"You didn't fail at anything," Dan says. "None of what happened was your fault."

"I'm not having this conversation. It's over. I've moved on."

"Have you?"

"I have." My jaw ticks. "Now drop it."

"Consider it dropped."

I know the guys are looking out for me. I'd do the same for them. My ex-girlfriend shattered my heart and ran away with the pieces. I'd tried to fuck the memories away, did the whole different-girl-every-night thing. Nothing worked. If anything, random slutty women only reminded me of the she-devil more.

So I swore off women altogether. I threw myself into work, got my administrator's degree, and today I landed my dream job.

I'm finally on the upswing.

My eyes lock with Raegan across the room and the smile spreads across my face. It's been a while since I've felt drawn to a woman like this. A connection. She's a sign of all the good that's about to come my way. Maybe it's time to break my dry spell.

Dan takes the beer bottle out of my grip. "Stop creeping and go dance with her."

I shrug off my jacket and roll up my sleeves until they're halfway up my forearms. Raegan watches me as I make my way through the crowd. Anticipation dances in her eyes and I can tell she wants me as much as I want her.

Tonight, I'm letting go of the past. I'm dropping the pain and heartache like an anchor, and I'm abandoning ship.

Everything's about to change.

I slide behind Raegan and wrap my arms around her waist. She pushes her ass against me and moves her hips to the beat.

"Your friends are watching us," I whisper in her ear.

"So are yours."

"Guess we'd better give them a good show then."

Her cheeks flush, but her arms lift, weaving her fingers through my hair. She lays her head back onto my chest exposing her neck. I graze my lips against her silky skin and her grip on my hair tightens. She smells like a Caribbean vacation, coconut and pineapple.

We're swaying much slower than the music, oblivious in our own private bubble. Raegan tilts her head up and spears me with those green eyes—not a bright, emerald green, but a deeper, muted green. Like a forest. A forest where I could lie in the grass and lose myself for hours.

Her lips part and she pulls me down to them. When we kiss, it's as if the power in the room goes out. Everything's dark and all I can focus on is the way Raegan's luscious lips feel on mine, the warmth of her tongue dipping into my mouth.

Ever wonder what a man thinks about while kissing a woman? The way his dick will feel inside her mouth. Judging by the way Raegan's kissing me, I might be in for a treat. But I won't make the first move. If Raegan wants to come home with me, she'll have to let me know.

She pulls away, panting. "Let's get out of here."

And there it is.

I wait while she tells her friends. Then, taking her hand in mine, I barrel through the crowd like a freight train that's gone off the rails. Or at least, I'm moving as fast as I can with the throbbing hard-on in my pants.

When we reach my car outside, I push Raegan against the passenger door and claim her mouth again. She yanks my shirt, pulling the neatly tucked fabric out of my pants, and starts unbuttoning it. We're a frenzy of lips and hands searching for skin, like we'll die if we don't touch each other.

"Get in," I say.

On the ride to my apartment, it's a miracle I don't crash my car into a tree. Raegan kisses me the entire time, licking my neck, biting my earlobe. With one hand on the wheel, I slip the other into her jeans. She holds my wrist in place and rolls her hips, gliding my fingers over her wetness.

This woman is fucking my hand and it is the hottest thing I've ever seen.

I'm relieved when we reach my complex, because I'm seconds away from having to explain an embarrassing mess in my pants. I lift her out of the car and carry her inside my apartment, our lips fused together until I drop her onto my bed.

We scramble out of our clothes. I can't help but stare as she strips off her jeans and tosses her shirt onto the floor.

"God, you're sexy as hell." I reach behind her and unclasp her bra, freeing her tits so I can bury my face in them. She moans when I pull her nipple into my mouth and swirl my tongue around it. I do the same to the other one before trailing kisses down her stomach.

"I used to be more in-shape," she slurs, almost like an apology.

"You're perfect just like this." I'm not lying. Men don't want to fuck a stick. They want something to grip on to. Something to squeeze. Something that bounces and jiggles. You might be embarrassed of your muffin top, but the truth is: A man doesn't notice what's between your tits and your pussy when you're naked and his dick is about to be inside you.

I tug her panties to the side and skate my tongue over her bare skin. Raegan hooks her legs over my shoulders, blond hair splayed out on my navy comforter. Her hips buck up to meet every stroke of my tongue.

Did I say Raegan riding my hand was the hottest thing I'd ever seen? I was wrong. Raegan riding *my face* is the hottest thing I've ever seen.

Uninhibited. Unrestrained. She's enjoying every second of this, like she owns me and it's her right to take everything from me.

This is how sex *should* be.

It's not a sprint, a race to the finish line. It's about indulging your senses. A tasting. Exploring to find what you like, taking the time to enjoy every kiss, every touch, every movement.

This is what was missing from the random hookups I'd grown tired of.

Passion.

"Jaxon," she whimpers.

I love the sound of my name on her lips, the desperation in her voice. I drag the entire length of my tongue along her seam, circling around her clit. "What do you want, Raegan? Tell me what you need."

"I need … I need …"

Yes, I love it when women talk dirty.

"I need the bathroom."

My head jerks up. "What?"

She rolls off the bed and stumbles into the hallway, tripping over one of her shoes.

"First door on your right," I call after her.

The bathroom door slams shut, followed by the sounds of Raegan heaving into the toilet.

Awesome. My head drops onto the mattress.

So much for breaking my dry spell.

This was a sneak peek inside Hating the Boss. Continue reading here. Available in Kindle Unlimited!

MORE FROM KRISTEN

Hating the Boss: Book 1, Standalone

The Collision Series Box Set with Bonus Epilogue
Collision: Book 1
Avoidance: Book 2, Sequel
The Other Brother: Book 3, Standalone
Fighting the Odds: Book 4, Standalone
Inevitable: Contemporary standalone
What's Left of Me: Contemporary standalone
Dear Santa: Holiday novella
Someone You Love: Contemporary standalone

Want to gain access to exclusive news & giveaways?
Sign up for my monthly newsletter!

Visit my website: https://kristengranata.com/
Instagram: https://www.instagram.com/kristen_granata/
Facebook: https://www.facebook.com/kristen.granata.16
Twitter: https://twitter.com/kristen_granata

Want to be part of my KREW?
Join Kristen's Reading Emotional Warriors
A Facebook group where we can discuss my books, books you're
reading, and where friends will remind you what a badass warrior
you are.

Love bookish shirts, mugs, & accessories?
Shop my book merch shop!

ACKNOWLEDGMENTS

Thank you to my beautiful wife. Stacy, your positivity and encouragement are what keep me going. I wouldn't be where I am without you beside me, helping me and guiding me along the way. I love you more than life itself and appreciate you more than you will ever know. You are everything to me.

Mary Meredith, this book wouldn't have gotten finished if it weren't for you. Thank you for allowing me to bounce my ideas off of you and for supporting me the way you do. You're a great friend & I'm lucky to have you in my corner.

Taylor, thank you for making another amazing cover! You rock & I'm so glad we're friends. I can't wait to watch our books continue to soar.

Dorthy, Becca & Kara, thank you for reading clips of this book at a time, and then re-reading it once it was finished! Thank you for helping me power through my self-doubt, and for answering the same question 100 times. Your ideas & opinions are always helpful & I appreciate your friendship so much.

To my amazing ARC team & bookstagrammer friends: Your support for me, my writing, my Instagram posts, and everything I do means the world to me. Thank you so much for loving my books, reviewing them, and sharing them with others. Your daily encouragement lifts me up when I need it the most & I'm so grateful to have you in my warrior tribe.

Xo Kristen